IN THE SWAMPYLAND

IN THE SWAMPYLAND

JOAN BROOKS BAKER

FRESCO BOOKS

I believe we all live in a swampyland, entangled in brambles and snares,

and yet the swampyland provides and surrounds us

with its nourishing seeds

To Margeaux and my other nourishing seeds

Publisher
SF Design / Fresco Books
Albuquerque, New Mexico
frescobooks.com

Edited by Hollis Walker

Printed and bound in Italy
ISBN: 978-1-934491-91-1
Library of Congress Cataloging in Publication: 2025903571

Copyright © 2025 Joan Brooks Baker

Cover: A photographic collage of the Okefenokee Swamp

All photographs and monoprints by Joan Brooks Baker.
Some names and locations have been changed to
protect the privacy of those concerned.

All rights reserved. No part of this publication may be reproduced, stored
in a retrieval system, or transmitted, in any form or by any means, electronic,
mechanical, photocopying, recording or otherwise—except as permitted
under the United States Copyright Act—without the prior permission of
Joan Brooks Baker. Nor may the pages be applied to any materials, cut, trimmed,
or sized to alter the existing trim sizes, matted, or framed with the intent
to create other products for sale or resale or profit in any manner whatsoever, without
prior permission in writing from Joan Brooks Baker.

CONTENTS

I	THE BURRITO	11
II	A BUBBLE OF CHIC	14
III	IN THE CAR	19
IV	BEYOND THE VIEW	24
V	WILD INNOCENCE	30
VI	JOHNNIE, MY DARLING	39
VII	I CAN STILL HEAR THE MUSIC	44
VIII	A LINGERING SCENT	48
IX	THE SWAMPYLAND	52
X	IMAGES OF MY OWN SWAMPYLAND	75
XI	STAYIN' ALIVE	102
XII	THE SOUP WITH THE CHICKEN'S EYES	106
XIII	CROSSING OVER	114
	ACKNOWLEDGMENTS	123

In the Swampyland

I

THE BURRITO

When I was eleven I told my father how much I wanted a burrito from the 97th Street *bodega*.

"How do you know you want *that* particular burrito?" he asked.

"Because when I go up to my friend Debbie's apartment on 96th Street, I can smell the food from the *bodega* nearby. It smells *so* good, Daddy. And I can hear them speaking a language that sounds pretty; I want to speak it.

I started to hop from one foot to the other, which I did when I didn't know how to answer or know what to say.

"I just want to go over there, to the *bodega*, I just want to see, look at everyone," I tried to explain.

"What do you want to see, Joanie?"

"Oh, I don't know. . . . I want to see the world up there. And one day I heard them singing in the *bodega*. No one sings around here; well, you do, but no one else does. It's sort of proper dead down here, isn't it, Daddy?"

"So you like my singing? Okay, I'll just keep singing to you, my little lamb. What shall we sing right now—*Jingle Bells*?"

"No, Daddy," I giggled, "it's still only fall, that would sound funny."

There is an invisible line drawn on Park Avenue, between 96th and 97th streets; one side is apartment buildings with fancy awnings; the other, known as Spanish Harlem, a large part of New York City, is filled with shops, three and four story apartments, commercial buildings—and *bodega*s, like the one that sold the burritos.

My father told me, "Best not to venture over there; stay on your side of the street." I didn't know what he meant.

"I just want the burrito," I whined, the threat of tears in my voice.

My father put his arm around me and said, "You'll learn all about different worlds one day. But best to stay in your own world right now. You're just a little girl. When you grow up, you can cross any street you want."

"Why does everyone always say, 'when you grow up?' "

"You'll see. And anyway, how do you know about burritos?"

"Oh, because I go to a sit-down Mexican restaurant in Midtown with Mother. She loves chili so much. Don't you know that?"

"I forgot. I'm never sure where your mother is. She's always out poking around."

"Don't you want to go with her?"

"Not really; she likes to poke. I don't, much."

One day, a very sunny day, the smells from the *bodega*, a block beyond Debbie's building, were wafting their way down the street. My mouth was watering like it does when you tell yourself you're starving. You're not starving; you just want something *so* much. And this time it was the burrito. I had walked the six blocks up from our building on 90th and Park, then past Debbie's entrance. I stood on the corner of the cross-town street that Father had told me not to cross and I asked myself, why would it be dangerous to cross over this little street to that *bodega*, its name written in big red-and-white letters on its keeping-you-out-of-the weather overhang. I had a dollar and some change in my pocket, because Father had also told me to always have money—just in case. With unsure steps, I crossed the street, determined to get to the outside order-up window. "One cheese burrito to go, please," I said.

As I waited for the burrito, a group of girls came around the corner and started to make fun of me, "Hey, little *gringa*, so what you doing up here in that cute little school uniform and your dirty brown shoes? What are they called— saddle shoes? Must be for horseback riding. No horses up here." They laughed. "So what do you want over here in *our* territory, hmmmm? You lost? Better get back to your safe place."

12   In the Swampyland

I was determined to wait for my burrito, but I started getting scared, especially when a big girl threw a French fry at me. Then she threw another and another. From the take-out window I heard, "Burrito coming up soon, *espera*."

Oh, no, I better leave, I thought. Turning toward our apartment and walking in as casual a way as possible, to show a lack of fear, I soon realized the girls were closing in on me. My fear traveled to my feet and they started running, slowly at first, then as fast as they could, back down Park Avenue. The girl gang ran after me, laughing and calling out in Spanish what I was sure were mean words about a lost little *gringa*.

Doormen usually stand at their buildings' front entrances under the awnings. From these lookouts, they observe the world going by. I thought that at least one of the doormen I passed would help me, but they didn't, and one even joined in with the girls' laughter. Finally, on 91st Street, Julio, our kind apartment doorman, saw me and the gang running after me. He ran up the street yelling something in Spanish. They yelled words back at him. When I saw Julio and heard the anger in his voice, I began to cry, I think with relief from seeing Julio—or because I knew I wouldn't be getting my burrito.

"Don't tell my father about the gang, he told me not to cross the street up there," I said to Julio.

He put his arm around my shoulder and said, "Maybe your father is right, sometimes people don't want you in their neighborhood. You can go when you're older."

"What do you mean? *Where* can I go?" I stammered, as I started my hopping dance.

"Ahhh, well, that I don't know. How about to the world? Yes, out there," he laughed.

II

A BUBBLE OF CHIC

"Some parents aren't very nice to us," I blurted out to my Aunt Billie. "Like Tania's mother."

"Come sit down next to me, Joanie, and tell me about Tania's mother. You know, even though you're only eleven, you tell good stories, almost as good as us Southerners," Aunt Billie said, her laughter muffled by her deep drawl.

"Okay," I eagerly answered. I loved telling Billie stories; she listened and laughed a lot. "So, the other day we were in Tania's apartment throwing water bombs out the window. I heard Mrs. Shields coming down the hall, and I told Tania, 'Quick, get down, get down, close the window. Here comes your mother.'

" 'What are you girls doing?' " Mrs. Shields asked in a low, angry voice as she opened Tania's bedroom door. Even though Tania's mother was not very tall, her presence blocked the light beyond the door, so she seemed really big. She was dressed in black—in proper slacks, not pants, as Mother would say. She had one hand on her hip as she looked down on us, crouched by the window.

" 'Oh, nothing, just looking at the people down on the street,' Tania said.

" 'I bet not,' said Mrs. Shields sternly. 'And what's that wastebasket doing there? You're not throwing that whole bucket of water out the window, are you?'

" 'Oh, no, we wouldn't do that,' Tania and I answered at the same time.

" 'Well, *don't*. I know we're only on the second floor, but how would you like it if you got hit with water from two floors up? That would hurt.' The telephone rang, and Mrs. Shields said, 'Oh, that's Armand. I must answer. Girls, if you *have* to throw water, just do it from the first floor, where you won't kill someone.'

We heard her giggling as she rounded the corner toward the telephone.

" 'Armand, sweetheart, yes, I'll meet you there. We'll just have drinks, good, I don't want to have dinner with those people. Yes, okay, darling, whatever you think. I'll see you later. Can't wait.' "

Billie looked at me and mused, "Well, that was nice. At least she really likes this Armand person."

"He's her new husband."

"Oh, and tell me what this scary Mrs. Shields looks like?"

"She's very pretty. Mother calls her chic. She has longish brown hair that seems perfect—not tight little curls—or that blue color that some mothers' hair has." I looked at Billie and could see by her nod that she wanted more details.

"Okay, she usually has a thin black cigarette holder between her teeth or in her hand that she waves in the air—like this." I stood on a chair, mimed her waving hand and pretended to smell the smoke.

"It's delicious-smelling smoke—the cigarettes are Turkish because Tania's stepfather is Turkish. The smoke sometimes makes a cloud around her."

"So, she's in a smoky bubble of chic, you might say?" Billie leaned back, blowing her own exaggerated cloud of smoke.

"I imagine her in the movies," I told Billie. "She makes me feel tiny and shy, and I want to hide inside my uniform and throw my dirty school shoes in the garbage. I want to say something to her, but nothing ever comes out except, 'Yes, I'm okay, school is nice, yes.' " I looked at Billie, hoping for some sort of sympathy. "I stare at Mrs. Shields a lot, maybe because she's so pretty or because she's so scary.

"You're pretty, too, Aunt Billie. You don't usually wear those pearls, though. Are they real?" I asked.

"Yes, they are, why are you asking? Your grandmother gave them to me."

"I just like to look at things, jewelry, stuff like that. Can I put them on?"

"Not right now," she answered, knitting her brows. "So let's go back to Mrs. Shields. Some people can make one feel shy or frightened. Maybe they're just scared . . . of themselves, probably. What does Tania feel about her mother?"

A Bubble of Chic   15

"Well, something happened a few months ago in their apartment when I was over there after school. No one was home. So, it was a great time for spying around the house—they call it a *maisonette*—with its own entrance on Fifth Avenue. I'm *really* a spy, you know, Aunt Billie, did I ever tell you that?"

"No, but I like spies. Go on."

"Okay, Tania and I wandered from room to room. We went up the long winding staircase to the bedroom floor into her parents' room. Her stepfather's hair tonic had made a stain on his pillow; she said it was his oil from Istanbul. That was sort of gross, I thought.

" 'Anyway,' Tania said, 'Come in here, into Mother's closet. Hurry, I want to show you something.' There were so many dresses—long and short—all different, mostly on hangers. Next to them were pants, then fancy silk shirts and scarves were laid out neatly. Shoes, every color with different heels, were hooked over the shoe racks. The whole closet smelled of delicious perfume.

"I didn't know why we were in the closet but I liked touching everything. Tania started rummaging around. She wanted to find something, but didn't say what. She was in a hurry, pushing through the clothes to get to the back of the closet, and then I saw her reach into a full-of-stuff drawer.

" 'Here it is,' Tania said. 'I haven't shown this to anyone else.' She held up a loose page from a newspaper. The headline said, *Scandal Sheet—Spring, 1955* in big type. "An affair" was written above the picture of her mother, whose name then was Mrs. Armstrong. The black-and-white photo showed her mother smiling, arm in arm with Armand Shields. He was handsome, foreign-looking. Words like 'romantic,' and 'a glamorous affair' were part of the caption under the pictures. Then a photo underneath those showed Tania's real father. He looked sad, and the words 'Broken Family' were written above his photograph.

"Tania didn't say much or why she wanted me to see this paper. I felt bad, Aunt Billie. I think Tania was crying when she put the paper back in the drawer. She didn't look at me, she just ran out of the closet and said, 'Let's go throw some more water bombs.' "

I waited for Billie to say something. I wasn't sure I should have told her so much. "Should I have said something to Tania?" I asked nervously.

"What would you have said?"

"I don't know. She's my best friend."

Billie frowned. "Tania sounds very hurt. She probably misses her father. What's the matter with parents? They make their children sad. Does Mrs. Shields take care of Tania? Is she always so unfriendly?"

I looked at Billie and hesitated. "Maybe Mrs. Shields doesn't like children. But she was nice the other day," I added quickly.

"Why was she so nice?" Billie said.

"Remember I told you there's a winding staircase up to the second floor? Well, Tania and I always try to slide down the banister, which is really hard because it's not the sliding kind. So a couple of weeks ago I was getting on the banister when suddenly Mrs. Shields appeared at the bottom of the stairs. She looked up at me and her face was really mad. 'What are you doing, Joanie?' she yelled. 'Where's Tania? Stop that.' Her voice frightened me so much that I stumbled off the banister, missed the step and fell down the rest of the stairs, landing almost at Mrs. Shields's feet. We just stared at each other for a minute. I thought, Oh no, oh no, she'll be really mad."

Billie fell out laughing. "Oh . . . I can just see it, what a sight, the Bubble of Chic staring down at you."

I wondered why Billie was laughing so hard.

"And then what happened?" Billie asked.

"Well, at first Mrs. Shields just stood there. I didn't know what to say. But then she smiled and kind of picked me up, arranging my sweater. For a long time she just looked at me but then she put her hand on my cheek and asked in a low voice that surprised me—even scared me, Aunt Billie—'Are you all right, Joanie?' Then she gave me a hug. It wasn't a big hug, but a hug, you know, and then she said, 'Let's find Tania, we need to go out, we need ice cream.'

"But Billie, it was so weird; a minute later she turned into Mrs. Shields again."

"You mean the scary Mrs. Shields, just like that?"

"Yes."

Billie got up and looked out the window.

A Bubble of Chic

"So, she became the scary Mrs. Shields. I think I know what you mean. We humans, we're so complicated. You'll understand that one day, Joanie."

"Why do grownups always say, 'You'll understand one day?' " I asked, feeling left out.

Aunt Billie looked at me, and just like Mrs. Shields, came over and put her hand on my cheek. Her face close to mine, she almost whispered, "I don't know why we grownups do things and say things. I wish I could tell you, but I just don't know, Joanie."

III

IN THE CAR

A rare treat, a family dinner at a fancy New York restaurant, was planned for that night, just the four of us—Father, Mother, my sister Alice, or little Alice, as Father called her, and me. Father had made dinner reservations this time; he usually didn't, which would often result in a sad, "no more seating for an hour" disappointment.

I had dressed up in my new party dress. I waited, ready, standing at my usual spot—my wide-open bedroom window—gazing at the sweep of soft rain falling on the pedestrians in the early evening rush hour. Steam, hotter than the heavy air, rose up from the sidewalk. Dusk was a particularly good time for people-watching as the hurried crowd crossed Park Avenue and waited on the median—hesitating, calculating whether they could make it across the next two lanes before the approaching cars, or before a heavier downpour started.

Father called out from the hall. "Let's go; the garage brought the car around; it's parked downstairs." I heard the coat closet door open as he retrieved his summer hat. "Come on, I don't want a ticket, and I have to stop for an errand before we go to dinner." I shut the window and ran out to the apartment vestibule for the elevator's arrival.

Father drove fast, then slow so he could compete with the changing street lights. He made revving engine and squealing brake sounds to make us laugh.

"Oh, John, please just drive," Mother said with a bit of an irritated laugh, but my parents seemed in good moods that night, so Alice and I hoped for a non-bickering evening.

Ten minutes later we pulled over and parked at the curb of 71st Street and Third Avenue. Father turned to all of us. "I'm running up to my secretary's brother's apartment right over there. He needs help with a letter to Immigration. I'll be back in fifteen minutes, no longer. Lock the doors and turn on the radio—Lawrence Welk is on with his band."

"Oh, no, Daddy, we don't like him; he's awful," I said.

"Now, Joanie," he said with a chuckle, "we do like him. He's smooth, makes you feel sweet and good, especially in this heat."

With the window down, Mother urgently called out to Father as he tried to fast-step away. "Hurry, John. I don't like us parked at this place. It's grimy. Why do you have to go see this person now? And the car's air conditioning is hardly working."

"It's okay, you'll be fine. But, yes, I'll hurry."

The tension, the fights that started with a gesture, a word, a laugh at the wrong moment, seemed to be in the air as Father left. Usually, as children do, we thought their fights might be our fault. It took me years to recognize that the source of irritation in Mother's tone, sometimes aimed at us, was meant for Father. Now I know that as we sat in the hot car, parked on that dreary curb, Mother imagined Father *not* going to his 'secretary's brother's apartment' at all, but instead toward a quick flirtation.

I had learned how to get out of the way. Sometimes Mother seemed to be spinning with anger, and we didn't know where it would land. Father would order Mother, "Alice, take a Miltown," the popular tranquilizer of the day.

The hazy drizzle gave Third Avenue an eerie somberness. We were parked alongside, almost under, the Third Avenue "El" train, whose clanking beat I liked. Passing trains created shadows on the sidewalk; they looked like monsters, and Alice and I giggled at their creeping movements. Mostly the city didn't scare me. I liked to stare at the people, at what they wore, especially their hats, how they walked, and if they smiled or frowned at each other.

Mother turned to us in the back seat. "Come on, children; we'll look out the window and talk about the people out there. You like that, don't you, Joanie?" She switched on the radio, but I knew she didn't like Mr. Welk, either; she just wanted to distract us—or herself.

We were quiet for a while until Alice said loudly, "Look, Joanie! Look at him, that mean man pulling the dog so hard."

I rolled down the window and yelled, "Don't do that, you bad old man!"

"Joanie, stop that! Shut your window," said Mother sharply, pressing her fingertips to her temples, a gesture she did a lot. "That loud train. I hate the noise. And don't kick the back of my seat."

She turned to us with a scowl on her face and said out of the blue, "And girls, don't talk to strangers. Bad people are out there. The city's not safe for little girls. And I'm really talking to you, Joanie."

"Why me? I don't talk to strangers. Who said I do? Maybe it's Alice who talks to strangers."

"No, it's you, Joanie," Mother insisted. "Alice's older, and she knows better. Yesterday, when we were on Lexington Avenue, buying that cherry pie around the corner, you stopped a man with a big dog. I know you wanted to say hello to the dog, but the man just didn't look agreeable."

"But if the dog is nice, the man should be nice." I sat still with my hands in my lap, wondering why I had annoyed her. "And you talk to strangers, too. I've seen you. And you're not scared of the subway, either. Sometimes you pray down there. You told me that, too."

Mother laughed, and turned around to pat my cheek.

I laid my forehead against the car's window and wondered why the glass remained cool in the heat. "Why can't I open the window?" I asked. "I want the raindrops to splatter inside."

"You should keep the window closed because it's dangerous out there, that's why," Mother replied testily. When Mother got mad, I didn't think she looked so pretty anymore. "See those men pushing each other, going in the bar?"

"Yeah, maybe they're all going to get drunk," Alice said with a slur that made me laugh.

Mother rummaged in her handbag and pulled out a handkerchief. She always felt better with a handkerchief in her hand. She shimmied herself over to the driver's seat. "I have the keys right here. We could drive around the block."

In the Car

"But then Father won't find us," Alice said with a rising sob.

Mother's two hands gripped the wheel. Her mood had changed, as it often did. She turned with a terrible frown to look straight at me, and said in that scary voice, "Joanie, now listen to me: You're only nine. You're a friendly little girl—sometimes too friendly—and you want to talk to everyone. But you can't." She gestured at Alice. "Ask your sister: she knows. Some people are bad and mean. Yesterday I heard a horrible story about a man who grabbed a little girl, pushed her down—a friendly little girl just like you—and did terrible things to her fingernails. He ripped—"

"No, no, don't tell me! I don't want to hear!" I screamed over her story, sticking my fingers in my ears. I started crying. I yelled, "No! I hate it when you tell me horrible things. Stop it, stop it. You scare me." I pushed her hand away. "Why do you do that? You tell me bad stories. Where's Nanny? I want to get out." I pulled the lock up and opened the door.

Alice screamed and tried to hold onto my leg.

"I don't want to be in the car, I'm scared," I blurted.

Mother reached over and pulled me back in, back into the perfumed scent of the sticky leather seats.

"Okay, okay. I'm sorry, Joanie." She dabbed at her face with her now-messy handkerchief. "I won't say anymore. I just got upset." She turned toward me. "It's this place, I don't know. Lock the door."

The three of us became quiet. Mother had her head in her hands but then called back to us without turning. "Don't you girls want to climb over the seat and sit up front with me?"

"No, we don't want to," I said stubbornly. "Alice and I want to stay back here." I squeezed my eyes shut. My hands were curled up in fists to protect my fingernails.

Soon we saw him. Father waved and opened the door to the driver's side. He waited for Mother to move over to the passenger seat, but she didn't budge. Alice and I were still in tears. Mother's voice, a mix of anger and relief, asked why he had taken so long, her voice rising in irritation when he didn't answer. "Didn't you realize it's dangerous here? Where *were* you?" She demanded. "Those men in the bar; they looked at the car funny. We were all scared."

"Yeah, and it's hot in here," Alice chimed in. "Mother wanted the windows rolled up so we were boiling and we couldn't breathe."

I whimpered, "I don't want to go anywhere. I want to go home. I want to be with Nanny. She'll make me supper. I'm not happy anymore."

Father was mad. We could see his face turning red, two shades darker than his auburn hair, as he leaned down to look in at all of us—from Mother to Alice to me. "What could have happened?" he yelled at Mother. "The girls are crying. I was only gone twenty minutes or so. Oh, damn it, why couldn't you take care of this?" He hit the top of the car hard with his fist, and Alice and I cringed. "What have you done, what happened?"

Mother glared at him. "How dare you?" she cried. She pushed the car's door open, getting out in one big lunge. "Why is it always my fault? And just *where* were you? You weren't with your 'secretary's brother,' *were* you?"

He glared back at her, but said nothing.

Alice and I cowered in the back seat. We'd seen her really mad before and could feel something bad coming. She turned and suddenly moved to the curb in big strides, unlike her usual ladylike way. Our heads out the window, we saw her pick up a beer bottle and throw it against the bar's door. "That's what happened, and I'm mad," she exclaimed.

Two men lurched out. They shouted at Mother, standing tall in front of them, "What the hell are you doing, lady?"

I cried out, "Please . . . don't . . . *stop*."

Father grabbed Mother and somehow pushed her into the passenger seat. I knew Father wanted to fight—I had seen him punch a taxi driver once—but instead, he shouted back at the men, "We're leaving. Don't worry. I'm taking her home, it's okay."

He threw himself behind the wheel. The tires screeched. My sister sobbed. I sat on my hands and closed my eyes.

"We're going home," he shouted to the back seat.

"But we were going out to dinner. You said we were going to have family fun," Alice cried.

"Your mother ruined the fun."

IV

BEYOND THE VIEW

In a yellowing old photo album is an image of me standing on our summer porch, arms draped over the railing behind me. I'm four or five, offering a big smile to the picture-taker. But my blue cotton dress had hiked itself up and my white underpants are showing. When I saw this picture as a grownup of twelve, my innocence waning, I was embarrassed.

But I loved that porch. It was part of Baker's Acre, our container of summertime. My father gave our mountain home this name and, although we knew it sounded silly, it was his kind of humor. The acre had a few straggly gardens and a big airy rambling house, but Baker's Acre was not really about the gardens or the house; it was about its soul—the porch.

I stayed on the porch as much as I could. There I was allowed to sit, read and dream without my father saying, "Joanie, why aren't you doing something?" which meant some form of activity, certainly not reading, even if it was my summer reading for school. But he, too, must have felt the magic of the porch, as I often caught him sitting and staring out into the meadows.

The porch was a world of its own, so special that it seemed more of an independent attachment to the house, living its own experience. Its area wasn't huge, but everything seemed to fit. A rectangular glass table provided the perfect place for lunch: fried chicken, cucumber salad, the best iced tea I've ever had. The swishing sound of the old, second-hand overhead fan could rock me to sleep.

The quiet snore of our treasured dog Popsie, his head propped up on a flower pot or on the faded floral slipcovers of the nonetheless comfortable chairs, gave the atmosphere a dreaminess. It didn't matter that the furniture got more and more beaten up over the years; it never gave up its life, just its springs. Several of those rattan porch chairs now sit on my porch, or *portal*, as it is called here in Santa Fe.

I had a big imagination, and the view had a mesmerizing effect, allowing me to envision a vast, far-away land, somewhere "over there." I knew that some of that view was just a weedy nine-hole golf course, but the extended stretch of rolling hills with a small but meandering farm in the distance permitted my fantasy of "way out there."

"Alice," I asked my sister one afternoon, "What do you think is out there?"

"Oh, not much—some hills and that farm, Metzgers' Farm. I've been there, it's pretty. Why?"

"I think there's a world out there," I said.

"What kind of world?"

"I don't know, but it's a big world."

"Whatever *that* means," my older sister of two years answered sarcastically.

Then Frank arrived. He was part of my imagined "bigger world," as he was German, the brother of Nanny, our caretaker/governess. Anna Hofmann was her real name. But to us children she was "Nanny," and Alice and I loved her with all our might.

"Where did it all go?" Frank had written to Nanny from Germany in 1955, not so long after the end of the second world war. Frank wrote that he felt lost, that everything beautiful he had known in their country was gone, had disappeared. "Our once-beloved country is so sad. I want to come to America. I'll find a job, I can do a lot of handy things, I love gardens. You know I'm a good gardener. Oh, Anna, pray for me that I may join you one day."

"Yes, I'll pray. I want you to come. It will soon be summer and I think the Bakers—they're nice people—would like you to visit the family in their summer home. That would make you happy; you love the country, I know. You and I, we'll talk about our times as children. We'll speak German—and English. You'll feel better."

Beyond the View 25

Nanny's note held a determined promise.

Frank arrived in the early summer of 1955, when I was eleven. Probably around the age of fifty, he was tall and athletic looking, and I remember the faint scent of cologne as he leaned over to politely shake our hands. His excellent English had a deep, gruff accent. All I knew about him was that he had survived both world wars. I wish I'd asked both Nanny and Frank about their childhood, about the wars, about the look of their parents. Did they give their children presents at Christmas or walk down the street for celebration parades? But the little girl in me was too self-absorbed. I just knew I liked Frank and I felt he was sad. It was important to Alice and me that he liked us; he could make us laugh with his card and magic tricks, and then a smile covered his sad face.

Soon after Frank's arrival, I saw him standing on our porch, which looked down on a sloping half-acre, a severe enough hill that it was never properly gardened. Someone had unenthusiastically flattened out three round places in the hill and had thrown in some seeds, but nothing ever grew in the unloved patches of earth, especially as one had to pull hard to get the hose close enough for watering.

Frank saw right away how he might help turn those patches of weeds into something more. Wishing to thank my parents for their hospitality, he asked, "I think I can bring beauty to that hill. May I start by making a walking path down to the dirt road below?"

I watched him create the path. He placed a log across a four-foot span of dirt rubble, then smoothed down the dirt around the log, packing it in to stop the summer rain's erosion. I could see a step begin to form. I remember how he protected moss areas to the side of the path. "You can take a nap there," he said. "I'll make it an even bigger place, you'll see. At my home it was damp like here and we had many moss beds." Frank was careful and precise, taking his time, looking and pondering, but sometimes I noticed his sad, far-off look.

One day I overheard Nanny and Frank talking in the kitchen about the stream they loved near their house outside of Munich. They both wanted "just a little house by a stream one day. I dream of that," said Frank.

    I ran into the kitchen and announced, "We have a stream here, a mountain stream! It's called Margaret's Falls. Alice and I will take you there."

    Alice and I loved walking the fifteen minutes down the narrow dirt road to Margaret's Falls. The path toward our magic destiny—a destiny made especially for us, we were sure—was banked by blooming, bright pink rhododendrons and paler-pink mountain laurels. I loved to be within the trees, especially when the rain seemed to turn the leaves backward and a sweet fragrance surrounded us. If it wasn't a magic place, I thought, then it was a spiritual place—which now, in my older age, I believe are one and the same.

    Five minutes down the road's amble, we glimpsed a portion of the stream through the thick trees.

    "We're almost there, Alice!" I exclaimed with anticipation. But we didn't hurry—there was no need to hurry; we didn't want to miss the pleasure of pushing each other, squealing with giggles, into the ever-present puddles, landing, I hoped, one of Alice's white sneakers in the mud with a splat.

There it was, at the end of the path, a wide, almost-flat group of rocks offering places to stretch out on in the sun while we waited for the courage to enter the cold water. After a while, one of us would tip-toe toward the pool's edge.

"I have to go in, I have to go in," I yelled to the trees and to Alice, who liked to call me chicken.

"Go on, I dare you," she would inevitably reply.

"No, *you're* the chicken . . . you go on . . . you go first . . . you're older . . . oh, please, just go. I'll go next, I promise," I heard myself pleading. "But I won't slide down the falls until someone stands at the bottom, like Daddy does."

"Okay, okay, we'll go together," Alice said. "But don't splash me, Joanie. If you do, I'll scream so loud."

The hope was that you wouldn't die, that you were brave enough to withstand the initial icy shock, and then maybe you'd be a better person, maybe even a proud person.

Frank, Nanny and a picnic soon came with us. We used the stones for pillows to lie on in the sun, and then jumped into the pool. Nanny wouldn't go in. Frank gasped, "It's ice." But he stood at the bottom of the little fall's slide of water to catch us and screamed when we screamed—just to make us laugh, I think.

Baker's Acre was in Buck Hill, a Quaker community that had strong patriotic ties to the Fourth of July. Frank told us how he loved German celebrations, the ones with parades—his sisters in *dirndls* and brothers in *lederhosen*—marching down streets behind a big band.

"I wish I could see that," I told him wistfully.

At seven in the morning on the fourth, the clanging of bells and the sounds of bugles blasted from the horse-drawn carriage wending its way on our mountain roads.

"Get up; everyone get up; it's Independence Day," the people in the carriages yelled. Frank had helped us decorate our bikes the night before with red, white and blue streamers. Popsie's ears itched as he tried to rid himself of the colorful streamers intertwined in his collar. Speeches, costume parades, then races and matches in all sports started mid-morning. Coins were thrown into the Olympic-sized pool for children to dive in and find.

The big moment at the end of the day's celebration was the recitation on the auditorium stage of the signers of the Declaration of Independence. When it was our turn, Alice and I both had terrifying stage fright as we looked out at the packed audience—full of old and young—but we recited the names, and we got them right. At the end of the recital, we were given a signer's autograph. I wish I knew where my mother carefully hid that valuable document.

Frank sat shyly in the front row, tears in his eyes as he watched us on the stage. He jumped up after the performance to clap. "Now I think I am part American," he declared.

I could never go back to Baker's Acre as I have wanted the memories to stay as they are. But at times when I have needed or wanted to imagine a serene place, I have closed my eyes to see and feel Margaret's Falls. I'm sitting on a slippery rock beside the freezing stream, scared to slide over the drop of five feet into the natural pool, a vast distance when you're little. Or I see the porch and the picture of me, the four-year-old who didn't care that her underpants were showing. And I see Frank staring out from the porch into what I had fantasized was the "out-there-world." When I told Frank of my daydreaming moments, he answered that we must always have imagination and curiosity, even when things are bad, even really bad.

Frank stayed with us for a while and also worked as a gardener for others nearby, but when late fall arrived, he said he must return to his country. I overheard my parents worried if he would be able to put his restored spirit into something positive, into creating more beauty, as he was determined to do. Could he start in a garden or a war-broken house, or maybe in clearing a path to a sweet stream? I wondered if he would come back to see his sister, or another American celebration. I had a little girl's hope that he wouldn't forget us.

Beyond the View

V

WILD INNOCENCE

I loaded my 20-gauge shotgun, took off the safety, and tightened my scarf. My left hand reached for my pocket hand-warmer to help guard against the damp cold. I was ready.

At the young but enthusiastic age of seventeen, I was proud to be part of Father's hunting group. We had gotten up before dawn for a big breakfast and then a short walk through bushes and a bit of a marsh to our hunting location. This part of the lush New Jersey meadowlands was quiet and peaceful.

We came to a spot and waited. Soon I heard a light rustle in the bushes. One pheasant flew up off to my right. Then another and another. Suddenly the air was full of pheasants. I shot; everyone shot. I heard *bang, bang* nonstop. It was raining birds. My adrenaline was running high. I had shotgun shells in both pockets and couldn't reload fast enough. The smell of gunpowder was dizzying. I could think only of finding the target, and I knew I had shot well. For that moment, I was my father's child. Twenty minutes, maybe half an hour later, the shooting delirium was over.

"Joanie, go pick up those pheasants and we'll put them in a pile here," Father instructed. "Then we'll split the birds up between the hunters and the club's staff. They're beautiful, be careful how you handle them."

"All right," I answered. "It will take me a while; they're everywhere."

Four by the tree, one under the brush. I picked them up two at a time and began a pile. But I wondered, there are so many—how did this happen with only six of us shooting?

First I placed the birds on the ground in a gentle, somewhat impersonal, way. But as the pile grew bigger, each one became a singular bird to me, and I seemed to arrange them with more and more care, mesmerized by their wild innocence.

I'd seen the beauty of pheasants before when Father brought the birds home to eat, but when dead their colors were muted. Alive, the males' feathers were an intense gold and green, the females' creamy brown. Now, the luscious feathers were everywhere, ripped apart, ragged. This is horrible, but I must gather them all up and put them together or Father might be angry, I told myself.

Studying the mound of carcasses, Father said, "This many birds isn't how it normally happens, Joanie. The real fun of a hunt like this is in the waiting, watching, thinking about the bird's hideouts, hearing their rustle, and then feeling the excitement of raising the gun for the shot, the bird in flight—a thrill when the bullet reaches its goal.

"But this *was* exciting, wasn't it?" he added.

"Yes," I answered.

I kept picking up the birds and stared at the display. I tried to put the scene in some sort of order, to make sense of it all. But unexpected tears began behind my eyes and my sorrow was amplified by one bird's ever-so-slight movement. It was a twitch, really, and I knew that happened in a death throe, however, I couldn't help but stroke it, just for a second.

I was not much of a sentimental person, but this massacre seemed callous, made more upsetting by Father's friends' lack of anguish at the slaughter; instead they were congratulating each other. I didn't know what to say and I wanted to hide, especially to not show my tears, which might seem unsportsmanlike.

But later I approached Father—I had to—and I said in a quiet way, almost a whisper, that although I had felt the thrill of the hunt, all that he had mentioned, the anticipation, the understanding of a bird's movements and then the adrenalin of the shoot. . . . I finally blurted out breathlessly, "Daddy, this makes me too sad. I'm not good at this, I don't want to do it. Maybe I shouldn't have come. But I wanted to come, I wanted to be part of this. You told me what a good shot I am, and I love the beautiful gun you gave me for my birthday." I was babbling, without tears, but in a stream of words.

Wild Innocence

He looked at me not with a terrible judgment but with an expression that opened a gap between us.

"But, Joanie, you eat cow meat, don't you, you enjoy the birds I bring home for dinner, don't you?"

"Yes, but . . . but I wasn't part of the killing. I didn't see it."

"Well, maybe you should see it and know what life's all about," he said abruptly, but with a quizzical look of tenderness.

At that moment, I knew I would no longer be a part of his hunting world. I would be left out and even though I wanted it that way, I felt lonely.

I wanted to understand Father's love of hunting and I wanted to better comprehend my own bristling at the trophy sport, the power that man needs to overcome nature, and the faux heroic idealism we accord the hunter. I had read about the Native American who prays to the animal that gives up its life for the hunter's food. It was not that I expected such a prayer to be a part of Father's hunt, but because of the kindness I had often seen in him, I wondered if he had ever quietly spoken similar words in his pursuit.

Several years after the shooting incident, I began reading Father's journals, which described his big-game hunts. It seems unusual in that era, the late 1950s, for a man like my father to keep diaries, but I appreciate that he did. Reading them, I could feel his sensitivity to the place and the process of the hunt. In his pursuit of adventure, high thrills and trophies, he wrote of the land and its natural treasures. A diary page from Brazil describes the needed endurance, the challenges, and his sense of sportsmanship in the stalking:

A beautiful morning with the dawn so bright and the sun like a tremendous ball on fire. We were across the river, only an hour or so, when the dogs hit the fresh trail of the jaguar. We first dismounted and tried to follow through jungle so thick that even with strong men manned with machetes hacking and hacking, we couldn't make any headway, so we ran back to our horses—mounted and galloped through to the other side of the jungle. It was a thrilling day, for we hit a jaguar trail about 10:15 and the chase began. What excitement it is to follow those hounds through all sorts of jungle. Finally we arrived to where the dogs were barking under a large tree—but after a careful search looking up through the thick jungle into many trees, we were convinced the cat had jumped to another tree and given us the slip.

But, further on in the journal, I read words showing an insensitive side:

We got some parakeets today as they are so colorful we thought they would look pretty mounted in a flying position . . . they'll make pretty trophies. We resumed our walk and took a few shots at pigeons and macaws.

To hunt for the jaguar through thick jungle, difficult terrain, seemed to me fair game, while killing a tiny parakeet instead was an easy, unconscious pursuit.

Father's words when I was the upset young hunter picking up dead pheasants, "Maybe you should see it"—the killing, he meant—had stayed with me. I was easily confronted by this question when eating meat or wearing leather shoes, or a leather jacket, but one experience stands out.

It was in the late 1970s and I was traveling in the same area where Father had hunted, the state of Mato Grosso in the middle of Brazil. My Brazilian friend

Kim and his wife Libba, who had been longtime New York friends, and Louise, my traveling companion, sat in the Cuiabá airport's outdoor café, waiting for a small plane to take us into a deeper part of the interior. The patio was terrifyingly close to the runway. Though white linen cloths graced the seven tables, glasses of water shook with each plane's landing and fumes from the aircraft invaded our senses. Kim, an art gallery consultant in São Paolo, was a man with a rich aesthetic; art and beauty were his priorities. Soft spoken, he showed a nostalgic care for the land and its people by wearing a small stone around his neck that held his memory of a Mato Grosso native guide. But along with other Brazilians, he was also a large landowner.

While we drank *caipirinhas*, a delicious, intoxicating local drink, Kim got up and said, "I need to change from my São Paolo business clothes."

"Okay, we're here, nowhere to go, we'll just order another little *caipirinha* and get high on all the different fumes," I said.

Kim came back to the table in his khaki shirt and blue jeans, but also now wearing a holster containing two pistols.

"Kim, what are you doing—those guns, what's going on?" I asked.

"This is what we wear to go into our area of Mato Grosso."

"What? Why?"

"Because," he said with a laugh, "we may own the land, but people come to squat and if they squat long enough, they are permitted by the government to stay. We need guns to keep them off."

"You're kidding!" Louise and I shouted in unison, dumbfounded that our caring friend would shoot at what sounded like innocent people. Libba smiled knowingly.

"No, I'm not kidding," Kim continued. "We can't have these squatters taking our land. They sometimes come in droves, like a flock of birds, and they sit and wait it out. We have to be ready. Yes, it's unfortunate; we shoot."

I looked at Kim and the image flashed in my mind of the bird hunt with my father so long ago. Birds, squatters . . . are they all fair game, all justified killings? Was this a valid comparison? Perhaps not . . . but it felt so.

Our small, well-equipped plane arrived and we headed for the ranch, but an urgent predicament suddenly presented itself—the pilot couldn't see the ranch's landing strip amid the vast jungle. As darkness approached and the amount of gas remaining in the plane prevented a return to Cuiabá's airport, we anxiously looked out the windows for the landing strip in the thickness of the trees.

Murmurings of fear could be heard among us about priorities, excuses, wishes, children. I, too, thought of people I loved, but as I had no children, it was my future hopes dashed that I focused on. But I also couldn't help but think of the irony of it all: Here we were, privileged visitors to exotic Brazil, with our friend, the guardian against trespassers on precious private land—and yet we can't, in our fancy plane, with guns and holsters at the ready, get to the ranch. A fly on the wall would think we looked inept, even silly.

In the nick of time, or so it seemed, the jungle opened to reveal a long dirt strip, adequate for our small plane. We landed, with words of gratitude.

The next morning we walked a part of the ranch with Kim's head foreman, Carlos, and his helper, José. They explained the current price of cattle, the process, the way of life in Mato Grosso cattle ranching, while emphasizing our remoteness in the wild and the importance of the incredible ecosystem. The scents of the jungle were magnificent—sometimes sweet, often pungent; the air was humid and clawing, the atmosphere full of mystery as the flapping sounds of the macaws' wings and the growls of the howler monkeys initiated us into their world. We longed for a rare sighting of a jaguar, as I remembered my father's stories of stalking the sleek creature and the thrill of a possible shot. Searching the trees, I wanted to experience his thrill, but the jaguar knew well how to hide from us.

Kim showed his concern about the ranch laborers. He'd ask, "Are they okay; who is ill; why?" He knew some by name.

We asked about the squatters.

"Oh, we manage to get rid of them," answered the foreman in perfect English.

"Is there violence?" Louise asked.

"No, but there could be; they understand that. They are poor for the most part, some from farther up in the jungle, only a few from nearby villages."

"Perhaps this is a naive question," she asked, "but there is so much land on this ranch. Isn't there any way a small parcel could be given or loaned somehow to indigenous people . . . to farm, to ranch?"

"No, that is not possible," came the firm answer from the foreman.

"Oh, then tell us about the villages, who are these people? Could we visit a village?" I asked.

"Well, no; there is fear that an outsider's germs, even a common cold, could decimate a village," answered José.

"But no one is sick in our group," we answered.

"You don't really know if you might have a foreign germ," José added.

After a few moments' thought, Kim said, "Okay, well yes, we're okay, we'll go to the village. There's a little motor boat not far away and José will take us. Won't you, José?"

"Yes, Señor, maybe—if you like." The foreman then grew quiet.

I asked myself with silent hesitation, could we be jeopardizing the villagers, weren't we too easily dismissing a possible complicity with a harmful consequence?

Yet with no spirits to pray to for permission or forgiveness, as the native person might have done on his hunt, we soon got into the waiting boat and sped toward the village—peaceful interlopers armed with entitlement.

VI

JOHNNIE, MY DARLING

I never heard my mother call Father by the name Johnnie; it was always John. But there it was in her own hand writing: *Johnnie, my darling*, her greeting on fifteen letters that my sister, Alice, recently discovered in a good-smelling, carved cedar box stashed away somewhere. The letters were sent in 1929 while Mother was on a long cruise to South America and Cuba with *her* mother. It was odd for her to go on a trip right then, as my parents had only been married a year, but mother's mother was sick with cancer and knew her time was limited; she badly wanted her daughter's company.

The letters I had in hand were written ninety years ago, a lifetime away from my childhood memories of the image of my parents as the fraught, bickering fighters.

Johnnie, my darling was followed by words of missing, that in fact she longed for Father. I was mesmerized by the letters, especially because they confirmed the little knowledge children have of their parents who are not just parents, but individuals, *people* leading lives in another world that did not contain children.

I *do* have a memory of my parents as *just* people. I'd seen them dancing. It happened one particular night, probably in the mid 1950s, at an award ceremony party at New York City's Plaza Hotel when Father was one of the men being honored by The Boy Scouts. Alice and I were told to wear something dressy. I picked my favorite, a green taffeta dress with small roses on the hem. I wore my black Mary Jane shoes. All of it was new, and I was proud. I had planned to wear this dress to the final night of dancing school but my dancing instructor died a week before the event, so it was canceled. I told Alice that this was just another mean thing that our teacher did, to die like that so I couldn't wear my new dress. Alice said I shouldn't say that.

We went to the Plaza Hotel event and sat at the "children's nowhere table" in the ballroom's side hall. As the waiters came through our passageway, I stood up to peek at what looked like shrimp and a mix of green things. A delicious fragrance wafted past our little table. "I hope we have *that*," I said to Alice, who then nudged me to move on around the corner to count the glasses on the tables.

"Why?" I asked her.

"Just wondering what's in all those glasses."

Restless, I sneaked off again to look at the grown-ups dancing. I saw Father go to the adjacent table where Mother sat surrounded by a talkative group. Father and Mother looked at each other; his face had a kind look, not his usual I-am-about-to-make-fun expression. He held out his hand and she took it. I remember what they were wearing and that they both looked—I had just learned the word—"elegant." He was in black tie—a stiff white shirt and a black silk vest; Mother had on a long green embroidered dress, wearing an emerald necklace she loved, the one I had wanted to play with when I was allowed to poke though her jewelry box.

The band started *From This Moment On*, a song I had heard Father sing to Mother once, when her best friend was dying. He led her out to the dance floor and put his arm around her waist, tight like he did when he danced with us children. They put their cheeks together. Father loved to dance; he knew how to look good and be graceful at leading. After he twirled her, she easily came back into step with him. They continued their twirls around the dance floor and every time they parted, their eyes found each other's gaze.

This loving scene has always had a place in the back of my head, in a vault of sweet memories transcending my parents' fights. The scene expressed a rhythm of romance and togetherness.

I looked at Mother's face when Father got his award and saw a tender smile. But she made a motion that she often did—for him to stand up straight. Why did she do that, I wondered; it kind of ruined the moment.

In the Swampyland

It was easy for Father to initiate the giggles. That was behavior he understood and loved. "This life and one more," words he often laughed out loud while giving us a bear hug. He called me Cactus Pete, as he knew I was a dreaming cowboy underneath my little girl façade. And he called my sister, two years older, "little Alice" and made sure she would have fun learning how to ride her bike down the New York sidewalks.

Father took us children on adventures; we couldn't wait to scream all the way through the roller coaster ride on Coney Island, sit cross-legged on the floor with him at the Wall Street Japanese restaurant, go upstate to pick the Christmas tree, and definitely to be his held-tight partner on the dance floor.

Mother may *not* have had a great sense of fun but she was interested in whatever was "out there," not in their apartment. Maybe she had too many helpers for her to feel the satisfaction of the role of mother, cook or housewife. Instead she felt freer on the New York streets, in the small antique shops, the second-hand stores, anywhere she could chat and engage with the owners. When we travelled together, which sometimes happened, she wanted to stay at the small inn, the hotel where she might interact with others in diverse cultures. Once when I was eighteen, she and I were in Syria where we stayed at a rustic hotel near the Market side of Damascus. While we waited in line to enter the Souk's café that emitted the best smells both of us savored, she saw a man she recognized as a well-known world missionary, Louis Leakey. "Hello, I'm Alice Baker and I've heard about your work in this part of the world. Would it be impertinent for me to ask if my daughter and I might offer you a cocktail at our hotel this evening, just a few blocks from here. We're anxious to learn about your projects." She knew I would be game. Mr. Leakey said yes.

Father would have headed straight for the 5-star hotel, perhaps to the bar, to give or hear some amusing anecdote. His energetic twinkle, his big smile pulled people over: "You won't believe the story I just heard. It's about. . . ." OR, "Let me tell you about a funny incident, you'll have such a laugh."

In some ways, both had world views. They could have formed a solid union but the necessary steam didn't have the needed positive energy or bravery. I wonder why: both were proud of their Southern background; they believed in their family's Southern values. Both loved New York, liked to entertain, were sometimes amused by each other and by their mutual friends. From my vivid memory of their dancing, I saw they could like each other, fall under each other's spell. They could be considered a perfect match; she was shy, he jovial and outgoing,

I wish the two worlds had crossed over to a whole. It was difficult in that era: Mother may have had a big curiosity, but her curiosity had few outlets, especially in a generation that rarely honored a woman's own path, unless she was a "character." She wished she and my father would be seen as *The* couple," but his wandering eye and public belittling comments made that wish impossible. So she followed the correct path, the one with rules, thinking it a safe and rewarding road, but a road without self worth. Her aura of distress was often visible, followed by Miltown anxiety pills. Father's view was through a big, fun-and-more-fun, self-centered lens. His focus was toward success, hunting and fishing, to philandering which, at that time, was a given in a man's entitled world. His charm was expressed in enjoying every day with people whose constant laughing responses he needed. Her need for connection was based on something more related to her depth, perhaps to her soul, but she didn't know how to go there.

In the 1960s, at about the age of twenty five, I had a flash of a thought as I stood by the telephone in their apartment's kitchen—always a messy spot of pieces of paper with notes and numbers. I was in between apartments and jobs, and therefore living at my parents' apartment, so I was in constant engagement with their comings and goings. That morning I sat in their formal, rigid dining room for breakfast. Mother had gotten upset with me for something and then had retreated to their bedroom to do I'm-not-sure-what in the somewhat lifeless, no-connection room. Father had been fun and jovial, his usual mode of behavior, and then had gone off in his boat-like blue Cadillac convertible—always with the top down even in winter—to work. In a moment of enlightenment that morning, I scribbled these words on one of the scraps of paper as a promise to myself: *if I can choose, I will live a joyful, fun-filled life, like my father. Simple as that.*

"I long for you all the time." As I read these sensuous phrases that came from a person I remember as proper, whom everyone called Mrs. Baker, not her first name Alice, I blush with a daughter's embarrassment. I questioned sister Alice, "do you think they really said things like that to each other?"

I try to look at these letters through the lens of both the child and the adult. As the adult, I wonder what became of the young, longing girl named Alice, what became of Johnnie. How did they evolve into Mr. and Mrs. Baker?

But the child in me remembers their gaze as they twirled for a moment on the dance floor in an almost dizzying trance, when he saw Mother as his dancing partner and she saw him as her Johnnie, her darling.

VII

I CAN STILL HEAR THE MUSIC

In 1963 Mother and I were in Egypt, on our way from Cairo to Luxor. It was only early spring, but inside our hot, un-air-conditioned car the air was muggy, almost sickening. With one arm hanging out the wide-open window, the guide/driver, while uttering occasional moans, used his other hand to mop his brow.

Halfway through our trip Mother began a story that seemed to come out of nowhere, but as she recounted her memory, I slipped into the scene she described.

"Let me tell you the story, Joanie. It was 1932, when I was twenty-five, my mother and I, with several Southern friends, traveled on a cruise in the Mediterranean. Oh, yes, I was married then to your father—probably a good three years. We hadn't lived in New York for long, but Mother wasn't well and she asked me to take this cruise with her. Thank heavens I did, as she died soon after. We had spent a week in Cairo before taking the train to Luxor to stay at the Winter Palace Hotel. Oh, Joanie, I so looked forward to it—we all did. I'd heard about the hotel's exquisite garden and we just couldn't wait to dance that night under the stars. You can't beat Egypt for the exotic, the intrigue— just thrilling." She sighed.

"And now I'm so anxious to show you that garden. I remember it was full of the scent of jasmine, and oh, the band—they played such dreamy tunes: *As Time Goes By, Night and Day*." Mother hummed the tunes as she lifted her arms in a dancing sway, her head back on the seat. "Just beautiful—every moment of that night so long ago. I can still hear the music."

Mother quietly added, almost in a whisper, that there had been a handsome man on the cruise ship, a Southerner she hadn't previously known but with whom she danced that night to the magical tunes.

"He was such a good dancer. He twirled me, slowly, beautifully . . . like your father does, only—and I know I shouldn't say this—even better." She smiled at the picture in her head. I looked at her and imagined the charming man holding her in a tight dance embrace. I also imagined those other young women and men crossing the dance floor, full of held-in desire, which was correct behavior for the time.

"I know I looked pretty; I'd had my portrait done in black crayon at Shepheard's Hotel in Cairo," she said, as she looked out the car window at the Nile's fertile fields. "I had a new haircut—the short style of the times. I love that portrait. You know the one, Joanie, it's in our bedroom."

Mother, in her mid-fifties and I almost twenty, we drove to Luxor that day, some thirty years after the Nile cruise when she danced with the special man, not just any Southern man, she pointed out, but a tall and slender one whose eye she had caught on the ship. His reddish-blond hair, parted high up on the side, and his white linen pants and blue blazer, not the seersucker suit that many Southern men would have worn, gave him a sophisticated look.

And it was not just any night that she remembered, but a compelling one that had lingered in her heart with a confused yearning; a Southern belle who longed to fit into Yankee New York City life, and most importantly to be the one and only for her husband.

She did fit into New York, in her own way, and she loved the city with an intensity. Charmed by my father's boyish ways, his good looks, his joy and humor, she felt positive about their future. Plus she admired his determination to make it in New York after his father lost everything in the Depression. It was not at the beginning of their marriage, but soon after, that the loneliness began, which started with a deep wish for her husband's singular love—for she was not quite his one and only. Father was not a bad philanderer yet—as if you can be a good or bad one—but his wandering eye and flirting hurt her. I had often

I Can Still Hear The Music

witnessed moments of his quiet betrayal and I could feel the deep sting that had to be overcome by Mother's dismissive soft laugh.

"And can you imagine, Joanie, as I danced with this handsome man, he told me in such a quiet way that he wished he'd known me earlier, before I had married. Born in a North Carolina town near my own, he lived there still. He whispered that together we could have captured the South, that my charm and curiosity would have transformed a community like his. He stared at me with those lovely eyes, but I didn't answer, I just couldn't.

"But for a minute, just a moment, he made me miss the loveliness, that small-town loveliness of the South. I told him to stop—I really did, Joanie—but maybe it was the heat, the music, the gin and tonic . . . it was so confusing."

Finally our car pulled up to the hotel's front door, and two bellmen came out to take our luggage.

"Oh, thank heavens, we're here," Mother said over her shoulder to me and the driver. "Come on, we'll leave our bags in the lobby and go to the garden."

We walked hurriedly through the hotel's slightly rundown but still charming lobby toward the glass doors leading to the garden. Through the glare of the afternoon sun we spied its dilapidated green gates fifty yards ahead. I glanced at Mother's face and saw the beginning of disappointment, her anticipation turning into a despairing sadness: the garden, now overgrown with weeds; the location, where the band once might have performed, revealing an overturned chair lying under tree branches that had fallen across the once-enticing dance floor. But the scent of jasmine still hung in the air, the meanness of it mocking her memory.

The four o'clock heat seemed to intensify. We both wore thin dresses and wide-brimmed hats. On my feet were sandals, while Mother wore the always-correct, high-heeled shoes and stockings that displayed her Southern gentility. We stood in the garden for several minutes, neither of us speaking, but a sense of melancholy enveloped us. Mother quietly walked to the discarded chair and set it upright. She looked at the broken remnants of the dance platform and put her hand to her forehead. I stood back, wishing something good would happen to break the spell. She pulled out the ever-present handkerchief from her cotton sleeve to dab at her face, damp with the heat. She didn't cry, but I felt her body's sad weariness in the thick air.

After a while Mother stood up straight, turned to me with an attempt at a smile, and stammered, "We must go find a breeze somewhere. It is so terribly hot. I believe I saw the Nile's *felucca* boats waiting in front of the hotel. Let's hire one and sail for an hour or so up the river. We'll find a driver to return us to the hotel."

"Yes, what a good thought," I answered, with the hope she could escape this crushing scene.

The boatman had let out the *felucca's* two sails to catch the breeze. After a while, the evening turned a bit cooler, while still holding a heaviness. I stole occasional glances at Mother, who seemed to be oblivious to the river's spray. She sat silently staring at the water, her hands in her lap, her fingers entwined around the waiting fan inscribed with the name, The Winter Palace Hotel.

VIII

A LINGERING SCENT

It was late afternoon, a beautiful New York day. I was the last to walk out of my parent's recently sold apartment where I had lived for twenty years, since a baby. As I was leaving, I noticed the heavy wooden coat hangers in my father's hall closet. I'll leave them; somebody must want them; they're too good, old-fashioned, I said to myself. The hat holders were still on the door; I thought of his top hat protruding from one of them and heard his laugh when, as a little girl, I would pop the silky black crown of the hat in and out.

Despite my initial decision to leave them behind, I placed the wooden coat hangers under my arm to take home with me and quickly closed the closet door with the hope that the remaining distinctive scent of wool coats and scarves would greet the new buyers.

Now the hard part, I thought—to say goodbye to the doormen, to those who had been my friends: kind and gentle Julio from Cuba, handsome Tony from Hungary, and stern Erik from Queens. They were my caretakers and sometimes teasers as I grew up and struggled with bike-riding and meeting boyfriends in the downstairs lobby for a movie, a walk in the park, or a party. Julio teased me when a corsage for my first dance was delivered from the florist.

I thought of my adolescent years, when the throwing of water-bombs out the window was the most fun. I couldn't help it; the sound of the balloon's splat on the sidewalk—and once on somebody's shoulder—was too thrilling. One day the elevator man came upstairs to our apartment's front door to say the police knew the bombs were being thrown from our apartment and wanted to speak to "the girls." Nanny told a white lie: "But the children aren't here." It wasn't a real lie, because indeed, we weren't in the apartment—she had pushed us out the back door.

Years later, when I was living with my parents for summer vacation and the eighteen-year-old drinking age was in effect, meaning New York was "open" to me and my friends, I would go to the jazz bars on the West Side and 45th Street or dancing places with Stephen, like The Ballroom on Broadway. Usually much smoking and drinking were involved, and I would arrive often slightly tipsy at our building's street door.

"You better sneak in without your parents hearing you," Julio said with a wink.

My parents took us for the summer to the Pocono Mountains for "the children's vacation." While Father was fairly happy playing golf, fishing or watering his garden with a gin and tonic in his hand, my parents didn't really like the country, particularly my mother, who agreed with Woody Allen that, "Central Park's enough country for me."

So why did they move from New York to the South? I asked myself.

"Who cares that you're older; it's a terrible thought," I had pleaded with Mother. "Father loves sitting in his wheelchair on the street, talking to passersby. You still get yourself to the subway and you're eighty-four; you like the subway," I reminded her. "And you know all the thrift and antique shops on Third Avenue. Those people are your friends; they like you. Please don't leave the city. You'll live behind a Florida hedge the rest of your life. It's isolated, lonely. This is where you belong."

"Oh, Joanie, it seems time."

"No, it isn't time, I'm sure it isn't, and it never will be."

After I had closed the front door to our apartment for the last time, I looked at the vestibule between the floor's two apartments wistfully. It had witnessed so much: When I was little, my biggest excitement was to operate the elevator's wheel and try for an even stop at whichever floor. Now, I looked at Mr. Julian's front door across the way and could still smell the alluring scent of his Turkish cigarettes. When Mr. and Mrs. Posner bought his apartment, different fragrances, from their Russian culture, would waft past me. The whole world was right there in our building, Mother loved it, just like I did.

A Lingering Scent

I got in the elevator and pushed the ground floor button. As the door opened, I looked for the last time at the wallpaper landscape scenes I had never liked.

After my goodbyes to the doormen, I glanced back at the building's long hallway and had a memory of the little girl who was always running. With tears starting, I turned left down the avenue, where the new spring was underway. Flowers were being planted in the divide between north and south Park Avenue. People walked hurriedly past me on their own missions, unaware that I was saying goodbye to my former life.

After twenty blocks or so of drifting down the street, I hailed a taxi.

"It's a beautiful day. Are you doing something fun this weekend?" the taxi driver asked.

"Oh, I don't know, maybe," I sighed, looking down at my hands.

"Spring is in the air," he said with enthusiasm.

I looked up from my sorrow and surprised myself by asking, "Do you *really* want to hear about me?"

"Yes, please, but only if you want to."

"Okay, well, I just left my parent's apartment after their life there of fifty-some years and mine of twenty. I'm so sad. I had to say goodbye to a past, and it just doesn't feel good."

"Oh, I see." He hesitated and looked at me in his rear-view mirror. "Would it help to speak of some of your memories in that apartment? I'd enjoy hearing them. I could pull over to the curb and turn off the meter—for just a minute."

Unsure of his seemingly kind gesture, I quietly answered, "Well, yes, maybe, thank you. Actually, I would like to tell you a memory."

He slowed down, pulled over and stopped the cab, turning around to look at me. He had a sweet face, a face full of kindness. We sat at the curb, the motor running, the meter off for more than a minute, really for quite a while.

"My school was only two blocks away from our apartment," I told him in a hurried way. "When I was nine, my parents said I could walk to school by myself. I thought I was grown up. And my sister and I liked throwing water bombs out the apartment window, but one time we hit a pedestrian who looked right up at our fifth-floor window. He was mad. Then there was a time during the Korean War, an important air raid, I guess. I had poked my head out to look at the street. *Imagine*, the street was empty of cars and people. The policeman told me to get back inside. He seemed mad, too. I loved looking out the window onto the world.

"Oh, wow, I think I'm babbling." I laughed.

The taxi driver laughed. "You remember so much. I grew up in Hungary and we had to escape. I miss my country."

"I'm sorry. I hope you like New York. I love this city."

I sat back and watched an elderly woman slowly walking her dog, giving him quiet instructions.

"You know," I said out loud, "it's odd, but there is a faint scent of a perfume in your cab that reminds me of my mother. Or maybe I'm just making that up."

"Well, an older lady was in my cab just before I picked you up."

The cab driver turned around to look ahead, then looked at me again in the rear-view mirror. Smiling, he put the cab in gear and pulled slowly away from the curb and back into traffic.

A Lingering Scent

IX

THE SWAMPYLAND

In my struggle to understand questions of belonging, I have taken the liberty of expressing my voice through my childhood companion Br'er Rabbit.

My great-grandfather was shot by his former slave, a man named Will.

Grandmother told me the story when I was only nine years old: that her father, Major Cyrus Butler, the sheriff, had been killed. Almost a century later, with the help of the great trickster Br'er Rabbit, I learned why Will had shot my great-grandfather, and I learned how Will had escaped to the swampyland.

There was a time in my twenties, in the mid-1960s, when I had a need to understand my Southern background, how I fit in, what had happened between Great-grandfather and Will. Brought up in New York City, with dyed-in-the-wool Southern parents, I had an image of myself dangling somewhere between Yankee and Dixie, looking for a landing.

In 1968, the year Martin Luther King, Jr. was shot, my need became more urgent. My only road to knowledge was to reference the culture into which I was born, the South. Aunt Sis, my father's sister; she'll tell me, I thought. I'll go to Jacksonville. I'm in between jobs. I could start driving down next week in my old Chevrolet.

I called Sis, and after much, "How are you; I miss you; what are you doing in New York?" chatter, I blurted out, "May I come see you, Aunt Sis? I have so many questions. I have a need to understand my Southern heritage, who we are, some sort of truth, Sis." I was close to pleading.

I loved her answer.

"Well, I am just tickled to death. You come on, I'll answer your questions best I can. What fun, you pretty thing. We'll sit on my porch and smell the spring blossoms coming out right now."

A "meant to be" moment happened two days after I spoke with Sis. I had a visit from Father's nephew, Tom, from Jacksonville, who was looking for a Wall Street job.

"Come for a drink, it will be great to see you," I said.

He came straight from his appointment at an investment banking firm. Dressed in a blue-and-white seersucker suit, wearing beautiful new proper leather loafers, he looked good, Southern gentlemanly good, with a sweet, open face.

"I'd love to get to know my Yankee cousin," Tom said in a slow, lovely drawl as we sat in the small but pretty apartment I had recently moved into—complete with a great view—a glass of wine in my hand, a Wild Turkey Southern whiskey in his.

After a few bourbons, Tom rather nonchalantly asked me, "I hope it's all right if I ask how you feel that our great-grandfather was murdered by his former slave—his name was Will," I think. "Do you know anything?"

I was startled. "No, no, I know nothing. People from the South, they never talk about anything that might smack of negative history. Maybe not all Southerners, but certainly my parents, who, while loving New York, are still Southerners in their souls. I've asked and I never get a real answer except, 'Slavery . . . well, that was a necessary part of the Southern economy.' I once asked Mother if our ancestors were involved in slavery. 'Oh no, certainly not, not that I know of, anyway. Joanie, no one needs to know these things—and they don't want to know,' she would tell me. 'I think it best to not ask so many questions.' "

I looked at Tom. "Now, Martin Luther King being killed. What a tragedy: he was a catalyst, an activist, incredibly brave. He even said to Black people something like, 'Don't let them make you hate them.' Imagine thinking that way, Tom. After the horror of slavery, don't hate the Southerner, the White people? Amazing. So, I want to know, where do I fit into all that? And here you are and you've just asked if I know anything. I know nothing," I said with a short laugh.

The Swampyland

"The irony is that I have just called Aunt Sis to tell her I have so many questions. I'm going to visit her in just a few days. She'll answer, she'll tell me some truth, I'm sure. Do you know her well?"

"No, I only know her a little; she's a lovable character. And not in good health, I hear? Maybe she will tell you some truth; let me know if she does."

Looking for distraction, I got up to fill our glasses and began speaking from the tiny kitchen.

"I have a childhood memory of Grandmother telling me when I was about nine that her father, the sheriff, had an 'unfortunate death,' that he was killed. I asked her to tell me the story but all she said was, 'He was such a kind man, Daddy was. I loved him so; my heart was broken. Oh, little Joanie, that was long ago, no need to think about it now. Let's go find something fun to do.'

"That's all she said, Tom, so that's all I know."

"People want to make it sound romantic, don't they?" Tom said. "Murder, and a long-ago slave as the murderer . . . that's a Southern story, isn't it?"

"And what do our cousins in Jacksonville think about the murder of Dr. King?" I asked tentatively.

"Not much, to be honest," Tom said with a shrug. "They say it's just too complicated. Maybe we're all naive or just plain ashamed. But your curiosity has gotten to your soul, hasn't it?"

"Yes," I said. "And the South *should* be ashamed. You live down there. *Tell* me what you know."

Tom laughed softly.

"I don't know the full story, either. But I'm used to the Southern way and I love it there. Perhaps we've done a lot of wrong, but I'll definitely go back home after I learn my trade up here in this wild city.

"And good luck with your visit to Sis," he said. "It's true. No one really tells you anything. My family, they just rock in their porch chairs with a mint julep in hand and relate wonderful tall tales. They're really good at that." Tom paused, took a sip, and put his head back. He gave me a look with a hint of a bourbon-grin. With a sigh, he said, "I like tall tales."

"But I want some truth," I said. "Or anyway, I think I do. What scares me is that I may have swallowed the family's 'don't-tell decorum,' and I'm just fooling myself about truth. It's so elusive, isn't it?"

When Tom left, I realized that neither of us had gotten any answers. I looked out the window, watching him hail a cab, off to a Yankee experience.

As I left New York, I drove fast and far. That first night, pretty late, I started to look for motels. "No vacancy" everywhere. Finally a dimly-lit "Open" sign flickered in front of a dumpy motel. I drove into the weed-filled parking lot and thought, okay, it's awful, but I have to take this. I opened the door to the room and a bad memory faced me: I was about ten when my family and I, driving South from New York to visit relatives, had stayed in a grungy motel just like this, with probably much the same graffiti on the walls. But the reason the memory was so clear was not just the shabbiness, but because Isaiah—our Black houseman, driver and "everyman" to all of us, couldn't get a room with us in the Whites-only motel.

"Where will he sleep? It's so late!" I cried to my parents.

"He'll be okay. Isaiah will find a room," my father answered with slight uncertainty.

Alone now in my motel room so many years later, the memory of that event lingered.

Early the next morning, stiff from the aged mattress, I started South again, and soon I was in North Carolina. I exited the highway and turned down onto the "blue highways," America's backroads. Flowers, bushes, fields of fruit trees, pecan orchards, and rows of crape myrtle bushes were abundant, enticing me to get out of the car and smell the scents of the South. I found a place to lie down among the fan-leafed palmettos. For a moment I heard the soft humming of the chickadees mixed with the faraway sound of a banjo. Wow, this is like a movie, I thought, and I felt a wondrous hypnotic engagement with the lusciousness of the South. I wanted to be part of that romance. My conversation with myself at that moment, like the landscape, was lazy.

I felt good driving in this beautiful place. Soon hunger became a priority, and sensing a good café on the next small road coming up, I exited and there it was, the perfect diner: "Good Eats, Come On In," said the sign. It was a small and welcoming space, starting to get the noontime worker crowd, perhaps from the furniture factory I had just passed outside of town. On a table near the entrance, plates of cornbread and pecan pies, a waiting big bowl of whipped cream next to them, tempted all of us. Most of the patrons sitting on the round, red plastic, twirling counter stools took a look at me. One or two half-smiles came my way. I wished I didn't look like such a Yankee in my slacks and collared shirt, silver bangles on my wrist. I quickly sat down in one of the red booths. A waitress came over. "So, whatcha doin' down here in our little no-count town? Time to see springtime in Dixie Carolina?" She laughed.

"Well, honestly, I'm not exactly sure," I said with hesitation. "But I'm on my way to see my aunt in Jacksonville. It seemed a good time to come. Beautiful time of year in the South. I was brought up in the North but I've got a lot of Southern blood in me."

"Well, you are certainly welcome in these parts. Bet you'd like some chitlins, just newly made, grits, some sweet iced tea? That'll get you goin' on the road."

"Yes, that's just what I'd like."

The waitress is friendly, I thought. Maybe I could ask her about the killing. Or is it just being White that lets me ask her?

"You're so friendly. May I ask—I feel I could ask you a question."

"Sure, I'll answer best I can. I like talking about our beauty here."

"Martin Luther King was killed a few weeks ago. What's going on? Can you help me understand?"

Without looking up from her ordering pad, she said, "Ain't nothin' goin' on, just bits of trouble where trouble shoudna be. Yankees meddlin' in our business." Her demeanor had completely changed. She walked away, giving me a backward glare when she said, "Eat up our Southern delicacies; then it's best you keep movin' on."

I paid the check, took a last look at those who sat and talked in eager conversation, many having a laugh. I got back in the car and drove on, window down. That waitress thought I was just a snippy little Yankee. My body felt cold with naiveté. I should have known better. The old song *Little Girl Blue* popped into my head, and the words came: *Sit there and count the raindrops/Falling on you/It's time that you knew/All you can count on is the raindrops/That fall on little girl blue.* I sang those words when I was little. Now they really seemed to fit me. Who could I count on?

As I drove on, I had a longing to hear from Br'er Rabbit, the wily trickster in the Uncle Remus stories, folktales of African American origin from the South.

My parents read the Uncle Remus stories to me when I was little and immediately my favorite character was Br'er Rabbit. I liked the stories so much because they were about surviving, conquering fears and obstacles. It was always the smallest and weakest of animals, such as the rabbit, who through their cunning and wit would win against the conniving, mean fox and bear. Br'er and his friends were treated as easy prey, kind of dumb; but they weren't dumb, and the tricksters, especially Br'er, became my heroes. As a child I suffered from night terrors of the "monsters" that appeared on my ceiling at bedtime, but with Br'er's help, the monsters disappeared and I could sleep.

Br'er was very pleased with his tricks.

"So, lemme tell yo," he explained, and his talk took on an urgency. "This is what I learned from being thrown in the briar patch. Y'all knows the story, how Br'er Fox and Br'er Bear caught me good one day and said they were gonna cook me, throw me in the stew and have me for a big dinner. But I got their attention when I tol 'em, 'Okay, ya'll got me, I knows that. Go ahead, put me in your stew, do anything, but jes don't throw me in that there briar patch. They thought on that and so, course, not being smart like me, that's what they did, threw me in the briar patch. I looked back at those two good-for-nothins and I got into my laffin' place. I yelled out at them, 'This is jes where I wanna be, I know how to work this place; I love dese here brambles,' and then I disappeared deep into the brush."

Br'er started philosophizing. "I come from a long line of tricksters. And, yo gotta know this: We all live in a briar patch o' sorts, full of tangles 'n' webs, poisons 'n' creatures; thas life. The briar patch is the same as what I call the swampyland. But fo me, it was a good place, cuz I knew how to maneuver it. People think the swampyland is jes bad, but no, it's where we is, jes life, and you

The Swampyland 57

gotta find how to live in it, how to survive, make it yo own. I'll show you, we'll jes keep on talkin about dese here obstacles, and dese here solutions. Yup, whenever you're scared, you jes call on me."

Br'er told me all this—and I believed his every word.

Finally, I got to the border of southern Georgia and Florida. Highway 90 stretched out long and straight through Northern Florida's small towns, Grandmother's home county. I wondered what she'd thought about slavery. What was in her soul?

Churches sat on every corner; a billboard announced, "Love your man and remember, the bigger and taller your hair, the closer you are to God."

At first I laughed, quite a lot actually, but then I could feel the disgusted bubbles rise up in me. Who are these people, these churchgoers? What's behind their religious zeal, this highfalutin', tall-hair-reaching-toward-God look. Their determined belief in "we are good, caring people" belied the years of hating and oppressing Black people. Is the beauty, the graciousness and joy of life that I have admired when visiting the South, and often feel in my parents' personalities, all for show? I thought of the expression I'd heard, "The South is not a place, it's an attitude."

It was late afternoon on a Saturday and as I drove through yet another quiet little town, I had an idea: I'll stay overnight in this sweet town and find a church service tomorrow morning. There must be a Black church here, and I long to hear spirituals. I imagine the churchgoers will be dressed up; glad I have one nice outfit with me.

Down the short main street I could see the Presbyterian Church next to a very green park, and just barely visible to the left was a sign pointing to a narrow road where I would find the First African Baptist Church. That would be the place, I thought. Stuck on the front door was a note inviting all to come Sunday morning for the choir service at 10 a.m.: "Let Jesus Christ enter your soul. Join us, sing with us."

Why did I think I could just walk into a Black church? Even though I had done so in the past, was I now presumptuous, naïve, arrogant, especially with the murder of Martin Luther King so recent?

Still, I was at the church door the next morning at ten. People were filing in, women in fancy hats, men in striped suits. I was greeted in a cautiously friendly manner. "May we help you?" a man asked.

"I'm just passing through your town to visit my aunt and I wondered if I might join your service?"

"Come on in, of course you're welcome here, but you might feel more comfortable in the back, that last row there."

"Thank you, I appreciate your welcome." As I took a seat. I noticed a few other White people in the back row.

The choir and one dramatically low, booming voice started their singing with *Wade in the Water,* a yearning hymn I'd heard years ago in a Harlem church in New York. *Wade in the water/Wade in the water/Wade in the water, children/God is gonna trouble these waters*. Someone told me the lyrics meant an angel would come down to stir up the waters for escaped slaves to make a safe crossing.

The preacher gave an emotional talk about Dr. King, about how he knew one day his time would come, and then the choir sang King's favorite spiritual, *Precious Lord, Take My Hand*.

Leaving the church, I wondered what Isaiah would think of me going to a Black service in the South. He once answered me, when I told him I wanted to go up to Harlem to a jazz club, "Best to stay on your own side. I know you're curious, but not sure you'd be welcome. No need to go now, maybe another time." His words reminded me of my mother and her cautions: No need to ask, no need to know.

Isaiah told me stories when I was little. One story always remained with me; it was so visual, slaves lifting off from the ground, flying through the open air. It was said that if the slaves could summon the power of flight, they could fly home, perhaps to the Promised Land, even if their bodies remained on the earth.

His grandmother had told him of a slave woman in the cotton fields with a baby on her hip. She kept falling from weakness and thirst. Every time she fell, the overseer beat her to stand and work. She would turn to an elderly leader, a Black man nearby in the same field, pleading in her despair, "Is it time?" At first he answered, "No, daughter, not yet," but after she asked him three times, he answered, "Yes, my daughter, it is time." With that she reached up, spread her wings and flew over the fields, her baby still on her hip. The overseer couldn't believe his eyes and ran helplessly below her. The other slaves watched, then they, too, spread their wings and flew.[1]

I didn't understand: Was it true? Was it just a story? I told Isaiah I wanted to fly. He smiled, but didn't say anything.

In the car, driving further south, I sang the spiritual I heard Isaiah sing in our kitchen—always in his low voice, to himself really, but I heard him: *Deep river, Lord. . . .Oh, don't you want to go to that gospel feast/That promised land where all is peace?*

Now, on the road to find Aunt Sis, I wanted the captivating image of the flying slave woman to stay with me.

Every once in a while, on a side road, I'd cross over the low-lying black water of the Suwannee River. I was in a hurry to get to Aunt Sis, but the side roads were enticing. The afternoon heat was getting heavier when I saw a narrow road that looked like it led down to a piece of water. A couple of shacks and verdant beauty crowded the roadside. Suddenly, a tiny sign appeared, as if from heaven: "Rent a tube, float down our beautiful Suwannee." My car miraculously ground to a halt. I'm going to give myself this treat, maybe just two hours—why not? I thought. I'm finally in the South and it's so hot, so humid, I can hardly breathe. And I still have a half-bottle of cheap white wine I got yesterday, just in case. I stuck the bottle, my wallet and my little binoculars that every New York apartment dweller has—not for birds so much as to gaze into others' apartments—in my waterproof camping pouch.

I soon found the rental shack and I dragged the big tire tube they gave me down to the water. I happily arranged myself in it and began to slowly and dreamily float in the comforting warm water, passing houses with green lawns that seemed to spread out forever. Horses, goats and cows, just as hot as I was, languished under the trees. Soon I saw a patch of grass in the shade, perfect for a nap. I slipped out of my tube and waded onto the banks. I took big sips of the warm but delicious wine and laid down near the river's edge to look at the fields and ponder an imagined past life, a lost era.

In the Swampyland

Lured into a magical wine haze, I brought into focus not the blue herons that I'd read were in this area, but the veranda of a white antebellum house in the distance. Wooden rockers and an old-fashioned porch swing sat still in the heavy air as if waiting, while the three ceiling fans turned as fast as they could to provide a bit of cool. I could see two or three people going in and out of the screen door, allowing, I knew, irritating flies to slip through. I smiled, barely making out the slap of the door closing, the soft sounds of an afternoon's conversation and laughter.

I remembered a relative once giggling, saying it was the humidity in the South that gave you "Southern craziness."

"Hard to think straight when you're lookin' for a breeze—one hand swattin' those pesky flies, the other holdin' a cool mint julep," she declared.

I lay on the grass at that half-asleep time when reality takes a back seat and fantasy slides forward. In my mind's eye, I entered the door of dreams, of imagination, and saw the veranda up close. I saw it all clearly: my grandmother, and side-by-side with her on the swing were Mammy and Br'er. They sat looking out on the plantation's fields, just rocking, all with sleepy smiles on their faces.

Grandmother was dressed in white piqué, with three-quarter-length sleeves that ended in red and yellow ribbons. Her hair was tucked up in a conservative sweep, hair pins falling out a bit. Black lace-up shoes with little heels were on her feet, which didn't quite reach the floor. Mammy was wearing a starched, long white dress—just as she did in the birthday photo I'd seen of her many years ago—with a modest lace collar of dark blue around her neck. Her hair was neatly placed on her head; a straight part went down the middle. I could just make out her weathered hands as she straightened a loose strand of hair.

And then there was Br'er Rabbit, sitting easy in the swing, his big feet sticking out toward the railing.

After a while Grandmother got up, looked at the others and said, "I need to go lie down, just too hot out here. Y'all have yourselves a good time on that ol' swing. Mammy, I've lately been thinking about my daddy. Why don't you tell Br'er here about Will, the Colored boy who shot Daddy? See what Br'er thinks of that."

The Swampyland

Mammy told the story of the shooting as best she could recall.

"Well, yes, hmmm, yes, I was there that day. We got a call from a neighbor, a plantation owner, who said there'd been a murder nearby. He described it all very fast, that a good White farmer down the road had been shot. The neighbor thought it might have been a Colored boy, tall like Will, 'bout the same age, who was running down the road, and now he's holed up in the farmer's barn. And the neighbor told the Major, 'Major Butler, you being the sheriff and all, you best go on in an' get him. Will—that boy—well, he was your slave years back and he always liked you. Tell him to come on out, that he's gonna get a fair trial.'

"The major thought and thought, I could see it; and he answered, 'All right, I'll go in. He'll come out. Yes, he was always a good boy, that Will.' But I remember the Major feeling for his pistol by his side, just the same," Mammy said. "He told me to come with him cuz I knew Will a bit and might be of help.

"The Major, he stood outside the barn and called Will by name, told Will to come on out, he surely did. But Will called back, 'Don't come any closer, Major. You were a good man to me, but you come any closer and—I don't want to, but I'm not comin' out—I'll shoot you, I will.'

" 'How is it you have a gun, Will?' the Major asked.

" 'It was here in the barn, thrown in the hay, still warm. But not mine, I didn't shoot no one, no I didn't, but nobody'll believe me.'

" 'Will, I promise you a fair trial. I really do. I'll do my damndest. Why, I'm not at all sure you're the killer, no, I'm not. Let me handle it.'

" 'There ain't no fair trial for us Colored folk, y'all know that. Now don't come any closer,' Will hollered. The Major just couldn't accept that. He went closer.

"I was right there, I saw it. One shot went into the Major's head, and the other straight into his heart. Yes, I felt Will had made sure he'd aimed at his heart.

"He was a kind man, the Major was. Shouldna happened. But I know Will didn't shoot no White farmer."

As she finished, Br'er sat there pulling on his chin, thinking hard.

"You know, Mammy, I'm a tricky one. Yes ma'am, thas what they call me. And I'm a smart one, too. I coulda helped Will if I'd been there. He hadn't needed to kill the sheriff. I woulda directed him how to escape, easy."

"And just how would that po' boy have gotten out of that mess?" Mammy asked.

"I woulda told him to tell the Major that he was surely comin on out, that he was gonna give hisself up."

"Yes, Br'er, and then what?"

"Well, the Major'd believe him cuz he already said Will was a good boy, that he'd been treated fair and square by his own self, and therefore Will would know that the Major was gonna help him. Now, I knows where that there barn is, and I do 'member there's the swampy nearby. So, course, there'd be a boat or a raft of some sort somewhere close. You see, here's the thing, Mammy. Theys two things about White folk: One, they believe they be darn smart and two, that they be good people— God-fearin people—so I bet they'd believe that Will, a religious boy hisself, would stick to his word."

"So, what trick did Will have? That boy was smart enough, but he was in a fix," murmured Mammy, looking away as if to hide some knowledge of her own.

Br'er reached out with his big foot on the railing to rock the swing. He was deep in thought but chuckling to himself all the while.

"Well, I'll tell you this," he finally said. *"With me whisperin in Will's ear, he'd ponder the followin supreme advice, he'd get to thinkin: 'I got to be mighty fast. Plenty of straw near me, so I'll set to makin a straw man, put my own shirt on him, hat, too. I'll stick these dark leaves in here to give him some eyes, nose and mouth, set him by the window in a kinda shadow. Then I call out, 'Jes give me some time, Marster Major, I got to pray for my big soul, you knows I got a big soul. I'm comin' on out, but I got to kneel down right here to say a few words to the Lord, jes here where you can see me.'*

"And then while Will is fixin to slide down the hay chute, he'll call out again, 'Yes, sir, you sho were a good man to me and I do believe you will help get this good Colored boy a fair trial. Jes give me a minute.'

The Swampyland 63

"And the Major would call back, 'All right, Will, you do that. Yes, you were a good boy. I'll give you five minutes, then I'll have to come on in.' "

"You surely don't think the Major woulda believed Will, do you, Br'er?" asked Mammy.

"It do seem silly, but when you believe you have de smart and de religious attitude on yo side; well, yo apt to believe things. That's what I'm good at, Mammy, knowin where people's lil soft spot is, where they be tricked the most," said Br'er, hitting his knee and "laffin."

"And then how's that Will gonna truly escape?" Mammy persisted.

"Oh, thas easy. What the Major don't know—and should've—is that Will, in his time as a free man, got to know that swampyland real good. Knew how to survive it. That territory, I can tell you, is some confusin' place. You can lose yoself mighty easy. But Will could maneuver in there, might even have liked it."

"Well, I do wish you'd been there, Br'er," Mammy concluded.

On the sweet-smelling riverbank, the sun had lowered toward the horizon and the leaves rustled with a soothing breeze. All this and the long sigh of a cargo train sounding in the background helped me stay in my dreamy state. Br'er Rabbit's conversation—so real—wafted across from the veranda like a sweet melody. I wanted Will to escape. I just knew it was right.

But then my dream was broken by gruff words thrown down on me.

"What y'all doin' here? This is private property; don't you see the sign?"

I didn't want to look at this dream-interrupter. But I heard my voice dip into a deep Southern accent, one that he might recognize. "No, sir, I didn't see the sign. Oh, I hope you don't mind. It is so terribly hot! I rented this tube so I could float, cool myself off, lie in the grass—just for a short time, sir."

The uniformed trooper looked me over, narrowing his eyes, but he didn't particularly scare me. Being a young White girl protected me, I knew that.

"Well, you seem like a nice young girl, but to tell you the truth, I need to warn you, we've been havin' trouble roun' here."

"What kind of trouble, sir?"

"There's a murderer on the loose, killed a good White man. So if you see a Colored boy, nice lookin', kinda tall, but actin' sorta shifty, you get to the police right away. He's from these parts, he's roun' here somewhere, unless he got into the swampyland."

I couldn't help but look at the trooper and wonder why his uniform was so tight; must be irritating on such a hot day. Too much butter in that trooper's greasy grits.

"So you best get goin', keep floatin' on down our beautiful river. You'll come to a place to find the bus back up near your car, I 'spect.

"And now remember, y'all come back soon, ya hear?"

"Yes, sir, right now, I'm fixin' to go a bit further on, visit some of my relatives."

He turned his back and slowly walked away, gun and keys rattling by his side.

I waded back into the river and resumed floating, quietly re-dreaming and talking to the Suwannee: I've always loved that word, fixin'. Wonder what that trooper is fixin' to do now, oh, I bet it's something like this: 'Think I'll go find me some nice Colored boy to fix some blame on.' Hmmm . . . I mused, so much for my own prejudice.

I could suddenly hear Br'er, as if he was by my side.

"See what I mean, jes look at that fat ol trooper, thinks he's got a handle on de truth wid his guns and all, doesn't know he has to be savvy too, like me, jes to exist in his own swampyland."

I arrived at Aunt Sis's late on a hot afternoon, and even though Sis was dressed in a wrinkled cotton smock and scuffed sling-back shoes—revealing messed-up toenails that held only a little bit of polish from a long-ago pedicure—I thought how lovely she looked. She had a beautiful head of silver hair and an amused twinkle in her eye. She gave me a big hug and immediately said with a laugh, "I've got a good bottle of wine here, les just drink all of it, haven't seen you in so long and who knows—with this damn illness, just a little bit of the cancer, they tell me—what kind of time I might have left for a good drink."

Then she added with a smile and a nod of her head, "Why, Joanie, you're such a pretty thing with your hair pulled back like that. I'm pleased as punch to have a good Yankee relative, and a questioner to boot," she laughed.

The Swampyland

We finished the bottle and toward the end of an evening supper of shrimp, fried okra and pimiento rice with a side of tomato aspic, she quietly asked, "Okay, Joanie, ask me your questions. I feel like spilling the beans, if there are any beans to spill."

"Yes, Aunt Sis. As you know, I was brought up as a Yankee in New York City, but with my parents' Southern rules. You know: Be proper, gracious, always look pretty, and for heaven's sake, don't talk about personal things. I hated those directions.

"But I have feelings, and I want to un-confuse them. So, here's my first question, Sis. Tell me, why is the South so secretive? You know, I heard someone say the other day, 'Where there are secrets, there's shame.' "

"Hmmm, big question. But let's just start. Ah, yes, we don't like to reveal, and yes, shame," she agreed, nodding. "We only want to show the good side, the gracious side, they call it—whoever 'they' is. People believe that graciousness is one of us Southerners' best attributes, that it can make up for a lot of shortcomings. Did your mother ever use that term, 'becoming?' "

"Oh, Lord, I can hear her," I replied. "If I said something personal to anyone, she would pull me aside and say, 'That's just not becoming, Joanie, keep it to yourself. People don't need to know everything.'

"And I'd say, 'What's everything? I'm just telling a story on myself that I think is funny.'

" 'Well, it's not 'becoming,' that's all,' Mother would say. I had to look up the word. I guess 'becoming,' to her way of thinking, meant appropriate. But who cares if I'm not appropriate?

"Gee, now I'll have to look up the word appropriate."

We laughed; I could feel the wine drifting into that not-caring part of me. I felt courageous in my quest to find myself with the comfort of Sis.

"But here's my big question, Aunt Sis. The man who shot my great-grandfather, *your* grandfather. What really happened? Did they ever find that man named Will? Was there a trial? I heard he ran, escaped far, maybe into the swampyland."

"No, they didn't find him." Sis shook her head, absently smoothing her dress over her knees. "Yes, they figured he hid in the swampyland, never came out. You know it's a jungle in there, full of creatures, some pretty bad. It can be dark and treacherous, with a fog so thick to make you lose yourself, and people—even the police—they're scared to go in. But you know, I've thought about this a long time. It's also very fertile in there, things grow, all kinds of seeds, good seeds. You have to know the land pretty good. And Will would have known the land. Maybe Will even found a good survival in there. He certainly couldn't stay in that mess he was in. For sure, he was going to be hanged. Talk is he was seen once or twice in that jungle and he seemed just fine, but who knows if that was true."

So maybe Will *was* safe, I thought, surviving in his own briar patch, in his own swampyland, just like Br'er said. I wished Br'er was with me so I could hear his wisdom.

"Joanie . . . now's the moment. I want to tell you something I've never told, 'cause Mammy asked me not to. You know, she and I were pretty close, we just had a bond, maybe I was the closest of all of us children she helped raise with my mother. It was about ten years ago. Mammy had moved back to Jacksonville after Mother died. She was still full of life, but she was dying when she told me this secret. Well, it was a secret from White people, anyway. 'They wouldn't understand,' Mammy said, 'they woulda thought me crazy; I just didn't want to make trouble and I didn't want to hear them deny me.' "

"Deny her what?" I asked Sis.

"Deny the story I'm about to tell you. But, Joanie, it's important for you to know that Mammy *did* tell your grandmother—my mother—who always kept the secret, as far as I know. Mammy knew in her heart that your grandmother understood the horror of slavery, that it was *not* the Lord's intention for people to suffer like that. But your grandmother hid her thoughts, didn't dare, I guess. Wouldn't have been good for her to let her opinions out to our family. Our relatives weren't bad people, but most of them had their dyed-in-the-wool beliefs. Maybe that's what you call Southern secrets."

"Go on, Sis," I said.

"Well, as I said, they never found Will. You know the story: A neighbor up the road accused Will of killing a White farmer. Will ran when he heard someone yell out, 'There's the killer!' He knew that meant him; he was scared nearly out of his britches, of course. That's why he was holed up in the barn where my grandfather, the Major they called him, tried to arrest him. But they had no proof that it was Will who had shot the farmer. You ask me, Will was framed. I believe the neighbor who pointed to Will as the murderer had killed the farmer himself, then saw Will walking alone down the road and thought how easy, Will being Colored and all, to put the blame on him.

"Mammy and I were sitting on her porch in Jacksonville, a pretty porch where we could catch the breeze and smell the scent of her magnolia bushes. She loved those magnolias. I never liked them much—too sticky-sweet, claustrophobic. I can see her fidgeting, picking up her Bible, keeping her hand on it, like it was giving her courage."

"Oh, Sis, please go on," I interrupted a bit anxiously.

"Oh, I'm sorry, I get going on my memories. So, Mammy sat looking at me with her steady eyes and caught her breath. 'Sis, I need to tell you something before I go to the Lord. It's about your grandfather being shot by that slave. Yes, Will *did* shoot him, that's right, and it's true that he'd been accused of shooting a farmer, a White man. He knew he just wasn't going to get a fair trial; Colored boy, White jury—no ma'am, surely not—and he warned the Major, plain as day, not to come any closer, that he'd shoot him.'

" 'It all went so fast,' Mammy said. 'The Major did go closer, telling Will all the time he'd make sure he'd get a fair trial. So, Will was true to his word and shot him. I saw the whole terrible time,' Mammy told me."

Sis looked at me. "Mammy had gotten frail, but her soul was still so strong. She sat there with her hands crossed, and then she said, 'You know, Sis, I believe in the goodness of your family, but I knew that boy'd been framed, he just wasn't the type to kill; like your grandaddy said, he was a good boy.'

"And then Mammy went on, almost in a whisper, 'Sis, you heard the stories about slaves flyin'?

"I told her, 'Yes, Mammy, I have, we've all heard those wonderful, fantastical stories. And I know some of the spirituals had verses about flying.'

" 'Yes, those stories,' Mammy said, 'maybe they're dreams, fantastical stories, like you said, but we wanted to believe them, course we did, gave us strength. My own mother was born a slave. She had stories of the slaves escaping, finding the Underground Railroad, and about slaves flying. She told me about the need to believe, that they had to remember, that they had forgotten a power they once had in their African background, that all was possible, *had* to be. I heard tell of the slaves' supernatural powers. They needed those powers, we *all* need those powers. Even if the body is still attached to the earth, the soul or the spirit can fly, fly to freedom. When I sing the spirituals, I hear my soul going to a deep place, another world—those spirituals make escape seem hopeful. Yes, we *must* believe that we have powers,' Mammy said adamantly.

"Mammy kept talking. 'Lincoln may have freed the slaves. But the brutality stayed on. Jim Crow days. I never expressed myself about the Black powers to the Whites; it would just cause trouble. I didn't speak to you children about all this, neither. I kept it to myself. But I *did* tell your mother, Sis, I had to tell her. She and I had a closeness, just like you and me. I told your mother what I saw that day your granddaddy was shot.' "

I held my breath and leaned in to Sis.

"What, Sis, I'm listening, please tell me what Mammy said."

"Mammy told it all in a quiet way. She said, 'I saw the whole thing. Your grandaddy lay dead. I knew he was dead. No one was about, but people would come soon enough from hearing the shot. I went over and knelt beside his body, and with my hand on his bloodied heart, I wept. Then I turned to the barn to see if Will was standing at the door, but he wasn't. Soon I heard a rustling, and I looked up. Will had climbed up onto the roof. And this is what I never did say out loud to White folks, Sis, I never did say it, but I need to now: Will escaped. I know because I witnessed it. He stood on that flat red roof. A wind had come up, I'll never forget it, a wind so strong. And then I heard him. Will called out loud and clear, 'Is it time?'

" 'I saw Will spread his arms wide, shirt flappin' in the breeze. I saw him, yes, I saw him *fly*. He *flew* from that roof. Clear as day, I saw it. Don't know where he flew to . . . to the swampyland, to the Promised Land? He was *gone*. I stood there and stood there, tears down my face. Alls I could think was maybe the Lord had come to get him to a safe place.' "

Sis stopped, her face flushed.

I sat looking at Sis, not saying a word. Finally, I had heard the story. I felt disbelief; I felt belief, some sort of truth was before me. Mammy had seen it all, and Mammy believed what she saw. Why wouldn't I?

Sis had tears in her eyes. "By telling you, Joanie, I've relived the story, the reckoning with all those troubles. In my mind's eye, I want—yes, I do, I can see Will flying."

Sis paused. I could feel her remembering, envisioning.

"But, Joanie, I can't for the life of me truly answer all your questions. I try to let all that I have seen sink in; some of it I judge, some of it I put into my basket I call the darkness of us humans. Yes, as you say, us Southerners, we don't always reveal, we protect ourselves, carry the burden of secrets or sometimes just put 'em in a box. It's not good for us, I know, but maybe we have to live with our secrets, some of it shameful.

"I've had a sweet life. I just love it here, sitting on this porch hearing my neighbor Joe slap his knee and tell me his tall tales; we Southerners can sure tell a good story. And I like the heat—makes me feel alive. Smell the frangipani, the magnolias—suffocating sometimes. But it's where I am. I'm right in the middle of this, my not-so-good Southern past, my own knowledge of oppression that sometimes I prefer to hide. . . . But I like getting up in the morning in this sweet-smelling part of the world.

"So there it is. Have I answered at least some of your questions?"

I had to take a moment and a breath before I could speak.

"Yes, Sis, I think you have. And I believe Mammy saw Will fly," I said slowly but with conviction.

"Hard to answer just straight out like that, but yes, I do believe she did," Sis said. "I like to think there are spirits out there. I mean this isn't all there is, I'm plumb sure of that.

"Truth, what's that, it's a hard one, isn't it? There's no simple truth," Sis went on. "While Mother was sad and deeply missed her father, she pretty much knew Will had been framed. She was onto the lies White people tell, and she thought she knew who did the killing.

"She didn't want to stay on the plantation. Mammy told me one day your grandmother's feelings. 'Even if there's a beauty here, it's a rotten beauty,' she said. 'Mammy, I don't belong on this plantation. This is not my soul's place; the Lord knows something's not right here. We'll go, you and me. I'll have children and we'll raise them together. Maybe you'll marry, have children, too. Will took flight; well, Mammy, let's *us* fly too, in our own way. She sold the plantation to the man she thought was the real killer, not Will. She told me, with a big laugh—unusual for your grandmother—that she upped the price and put a little curse on the land. And then she moved away to a small small college town called Davidson where people were more tolerant and open to ideas.' "

After a long minute, I said, "Sis, I've been waiting for this moment. There was always something so troubling about my past, no one talking about feelings. All those pieces have been floating around. I'm struggling, but maybe now some will come together. Just like you, I believe there's magic out there, spirits; just has to be. But I need to go off somewhere to think about all this. Please excuse me."

"You go on," Sis said, patting my knee. "Take your time. Go on down by the river."

A river had always been good to me, good for my dreaming. I walked down to the banks of the St. John's River, not far from Sis's house. It was about nine in the evening, that late hour of a very late spring, full of light and heat. I saw some soft grass and laid down, closed my eyes. All those images: my great-grandfather's death; Mammy kneeling beside him; and then the image of Will, his arms flung out, wing-like.

The Swampyland

I thought of the swampyland—what is it, really? What about my own swampyland? Now in my mid-twenties, I'd waded into pools of self-doubt, feeling lost, restless, often making choices that rejected safety, but which had given me joy, astonishment and wonder—amid the brambles and the poisons.

I squeezed my eyes shut, longing for Br'er. He would help me understand my questions, I was sure.

Dreaminess began to overtake me, sinking me into my longed-for imagination. Several times I called out to Br'er.

Finally he answered, *"Here I is."*

It seemed so real. I saw Br'er sitting on the swing, chewing on a straw, his big feet, as usual, on the railing. This time I felt I was next to him, so close we were.

"Now whas troublin yo?"

I told him. "Br'er, I thought I was looking for truth, but maybe I can't recognize it. Aunt Sis just said there's no simple truth."

"Hmmm. Truth! Maybe it's jes yo own truth. Yo gotta go on thru this here swampyland and see whas up, to make up yo own mind. Sometime find yoself some tricks, like me with that mean ol' Br'er Fox."

Br'er looked my way and with that, he slapped his knee and got into his "laffin' place." I felt my own big laugh rise up from somewhere deep inside me to meet his. I stuck my foot alongside Br'er's on the railing and we pushed off together, waiting for the cool breeze.

1. See "Flying Africans" in The Annotated African American Folktales, by Henry Louis Gates, Jr. and Maria Tatar (Liverwright Publishing Corporation, 2018).

The Swampyland

In the Swampyland

X
MY OWN SWAMPYLAND

An image can tell a story.

We all navigate our swampyland in different ways. In search of meaning and resolution, we encounter joy, pain, balance, danger, beauty, comfort, connection, aloneness, humor, sorrow, love, fear, wonder, peace, and the unknown.

My Own Swampyland

My Own Swampyland

My Own Swampyland

82 In the Swampyland

My Own Swampyland

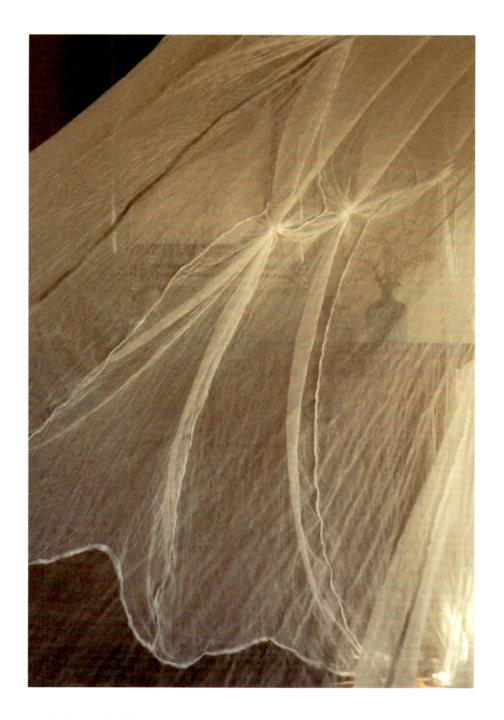

My Own Swampyland

My Own Swampyland

88 In the Swampyland

My Own Swampyland

My Own Swampyland

94   In the Swampyland

My Own Swampyland

96   In the Swampyland

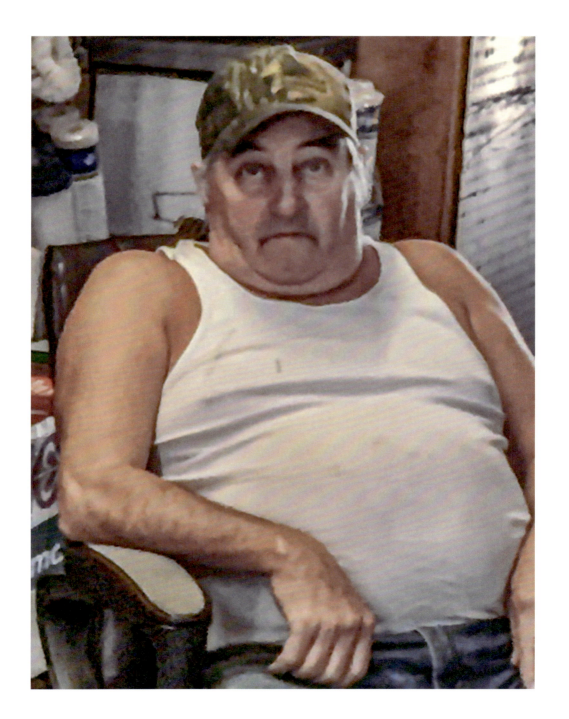

My Own Swampyland

In the Swampyland

My Own Swampyland

My Own Swampyland

XI

STAYIN' ALIVE

Walking toward New York's Union Square, the closest subway stop to my apartment, I ogle at the different faces: the Hare Krishnas, the striped-tied Wall Streeters, the chess players, the crazies; they're all here, coming and going. I approach the stairs down into the subway's grimy but fascinating underworld and hear the usual, "One dolla, one dolla" from the Eastern European man who sits near the entrance selling bottles of water set up on a rickety crate. He has a sweet smile that seems lost in some other world, and he says the same phrase over and over. One day I gave him $50. I don't know exactly why I gave him the money, but I liked this stranger, and maybe I just wanted to hear his surprise. But the surprise was mine; he abandoned his usual, "One dolla, one dolla," and, looking at me, he articulated in perfect English, "I don't know how to show you my thanks."

"What?" I said with surprise. Ever since then, I have looked for him every time on my route to the underworld.

Once down the stairs and onto the subway's perpetually filthy concrete floor, leading to all the lines—uptown, downtown, any borough—I move through the crowd, and with care, hurry down the next set of stairs to make it just in the nick of time for an approaching train, the Number 5 Express. Sometimes people even hold the train door open for others to enter. Often there's an unusual, though certainly not sought-after, intimacy in a crowded car. With luck, this burden of intimacy will not last long, yet oddly, an actual relationship might be forged, at least in the humorous sharing of crowd-suffering.

About seven one evening, late for what I anticipated would be a fine dinner, my high-speed subway scurry was in full gear. But a crowd waiting in front of six musicians blocked my path. Suddenly, the band began—loud and big—a song I love, *Stayin' Alive*. I turned to the band; the spirit of the music not only filled the air but also my soul. And right away the sea of people in front of me and I began to sway and move—I mean *all* of us, *everyone* started to dance—either stepping in place or with a slight lean toward a stranger. I stayed—couldn't *not* stay—and, with joy, forgot about my hurry to somewhere.

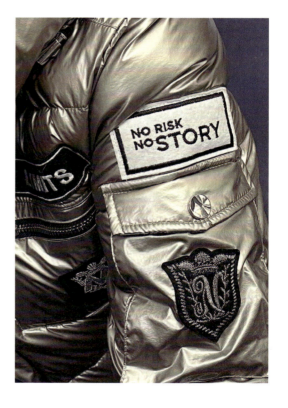

My mother, somewhat frail but still feisty at eighty-four, liked the subway too. She had four solid rules: Don't stand by the tracks in case some crazy person pushes you; look for a nice young man who is going to save you; carry an umbrella to hit an approaching bad man; and, then she would say with a smile, "Well, I pray a lot."

Yes, I've experienced bad things down there, but generosity, too. Years ago, I started off late from Wall Street for a meeting Uptown, but I hadn't organized the documents to be handed out. I held 200 unstapled pages. Near panic, I stepped into a train's uncrowded car. Everyone and everything was quiet except for my beating heart. I suddenly heard myself say in a loud, unsteady voice, "Excuse me, but would all of you please create a long empty seat for me; I need help. I have to put these pages into numerical order and staple them. I have the stapler right here, I do, I really do, see?" pointing to the stapler in my other hand. People first looked at me with a frown, suspicious, but a woman in a cocky green beret put her packages down and sauntered over. A man with a dog in his lap rose and tied the leash to a pole. I had four stops before I had to get off, maybe just enough time, I prayed, in a loud whisper.

We did it; we stapled all two hundred pages before reaching my stop. Clapping and smiles celebrated a moment of joy for an amazing accomplishment. As the subway door opened at my stop, I turned and threw kisses at my new friends. The man made his dog wave.

Another moment of interaction happened in the "upper-world" part of Union Square at the huge, two-day-a-week Farmer's Market. The stalls—mostly from New Jersey farms—are lined up for at least three blocks on the square's eastern side. I spied Marina.

"There you are, I was looking for your booth; you moved," I said to the gregarious cheese vendor from whom you could get a generous taste or two. I had gotten to know Marina a bit, and on that sunny day, we sat on two big crates precariously set up by the side of her stall. "So, what's up?" I asked her.

"My ornery great aunt just died. So this weekend we had a big funeral. She was sort of a mean ol' person, mean as a snake really; she didn't like *anyone*. But when she knew she was dying, she made a last request to have her body laid out in the casket—face *down*. 'That way,' my aunt announced, 'when people lean over the casket to kiss me, they'll have to kiss my ass goodbye. ' "

"Go on, make your move; yeah, move *that* bishop," said T.C., motioning with his finger. T.C.—one of the chess teachers on the square whom I strongly felt was my very own personal chess teacher. His reputation as king of the square amused him. From Ghana, he uses T.C. as a shortcut to his unpronounceable name.

"So what's T.C. stand for?" finally I asked one day.

"Joan, it means Teacher of Chess, of course."

When we're playing, onlookers sometimes suggest a move, but their comments irritate me as I only want one teacher. I grumble at them. T.C. laughs at me, sometimes with me.

He knows the square: the locations of the undercover cops, who the bad panhandlers are, which farm stand has the freshest produce. As T.C. concentrates on my chess lesson, he looks at me and pontificates, usually with a round red lollipop in his mouth.

"It's all played with a simple, brilliant strategy, Joan. And, of course, it is only *I* who knows the strategy." Somehow, he doesn't get mad when I make the same mistake over and over; he's just amused.

He sits, Buddha-like, behind his chess set, assessing the crowd as the all-knowing observer.

"So, what do you see today in this square or on the subway, Joan? You're always looking around. Tell me."

"Maybe I see the universe—best and worst," I replied. "It's alive here, all possibilities, all connections. Just think—Union Square is in a huge urban center but over there are the rural farmers. It's all a whole."

"Yeah, maybe the world's right here. So, tell me again about your mother, how she stood far from the tracks with her umbrella in hand and prayed. I like that vision. She got it right; should have met her," T.C. mused. "Okay, let's play. I'll teach you a new trick, and you can add it to the old ones you can't remember." T.C. looked at me with a twinkle, his lollipop rolling around in his mouth.

Stayin' Alive   105

XII

THE SOUP WITH THE CHICKEN'S EYES

The bus lurched and swerved as we approached the terrifying curve. With my eyes shut, I was grateful when we finally pulled over and came to a full stop. The driver got up from his seat and passed around a mashed-in tin box. All of us reached into our pockets for donations to the Virgin Mary, the statue that awaited us on the edge of the curve's cliff. The box filled quickly.

The bus ride continued for a few more hours' journey from Bogotá to the coastal town of Cabo Corrientes. Passengers were crowded in with one goat, three chickens and some unidentifiable creature with furry ears squished onto the floor beneath two passengers.

Traveling alone but not lonely, staring at everyone—my favorite pastime— I made up stories for each person: a farmer, a rancher, and a man with a jagged scar down his jaw that reminded me of an old saw. He must be a gangster going to the coast to pick up drugs, my imagination announced.

My seatmate told me he was visiting Corrientes. "Good for fish," he said. I told him I was a photographer, that I wanted to visit the sea, but mainly I'd been hired—although I was unable to think of the Spanish word for "hire"—by my American friend, Bill, to photograph his hat factory outside of the town. The man nodded. I probably said it wrong. It was 1971 and after obsessively studying, my Spanish by then had become only slightly acceptable. I wanted to communicate, to feel part of the world I was visiting, just one of several reasons for my journey—to be accomplished partly by hitchhiking—through South America.

106   In the Swampyland

We stopped at a roadside café for an early evening break. In the simple interior, three long tables were placed to enable the thirty or so passengers to sit next to each other and, for very little money, be served soup and bread. Still staring at everyone, I noticed how people sat quietly, their hands folded in quick silent blessings, dusty straw hats firmly placed on their heads, while I worried if I had left any crackers and cheese on my bus seat that the animals might now be enjoying.

I can still see the big bowl of soup put in front of me, smell the delicious scents of the vegetables and chicken broth. I began to hungrily slurp it up until my spoon touched something hard; a chicken's head floated to the surface and rolled over, its eyes staring up at me. I gasped, slammed my spoon down and looked around to see if others were having this same disturbing experience. Apparently not. Could it just be in *my* soup, the only *gringa* on the bus, or would that part of the bird be considered a silent gift, another culture's delicacy? I was more than startled. The eyes somehow penetrated me. Usually I'm looking out from behind the camera; now this dead chicken's eyes were looking at *me*; I felt them unveiling my secret fear of not belonging.

That evening I titled my diary page, "The Soup with the Chicken's Eyes." I'm not sure where I spent the night, still hungry.

I probably would have liked Corrientes, a pretty oceanside town dotted with fisherman's houses, but I don't remember a great deal about it except for a small street leading down to the rickety fishing dock, a street alive with the biggest cockroaches I'd ever seen. I still clearly recall the horror of hearing the crunch of them under my feet.

Being from New York City, which is known for *its* virulent cockroaches, I have an inherent repugnance for the dreaded bugs. They seem to survive in the best and fanciest of places, not just in rundown areas where one would *like* to think they lived. I once shared an apartment on East 51st Street near the East River. One night upon coming home I was greeted by a disgusting vision: the kitchen's walls were polka-dotted with cockroaches. My friend had sprayed bug repellent on the few she'd seen an hour before, but we soon learned that

The Soup With The Chicken's Eyes

particular spray was considered a delicacy by the roaches; now they had all emerged for the party.

We called the bug-remover man early the next morning. He came without delay, having heard the panic in my voice. I told him the usual New York apartment-owner's story: "They're renovating the apartment next door and the roaches are coming over from there." The man stopped and, with a hint of exhaustion and a frown, asked, "Lady, when are people gonna accept the cockroaches as their very own? These here cockroaches, they belong to *you*."

I burst out laughing and then asked with what I thought was an amused tone, "Gee, this disgusting scene isn't somebody *else's* fault?" I don't remember him laughing along with me.

Those two alarming experiences—neither of which endangered me—still remain fresh in my mind. There is something about the rawness of them both: The cockroaches seemed to have free reign wherever they lived, and the unmoving, staring chicken's eyes exposed my anxiety as a stranger: *What are you doing here? Why? Who are you?*

After the soup experience I took the bus back to Bogotá—without incident—and then drove the next day with Bill to photograph the wildness at a ranch in the *llanos* (the plains) in southeastern Colombia. It is an ecoregion of grasslands and shrubs full of various animals: beautiful and ugly, lethal and harmless. The ranch was owned by Americans I knew from New York and served as a research center for scientists from various parts of the world. A mix of people worked there, tending the fields and managing the headquarters. An American couple with a baby, and Luisa, the beautiful and tough Colombian caretaker, greeted us on our arrival. It was evening. Our long drive over the Andes, followed by a fast charge through a good-sized river in a ranch hand's truck, was exhilarating but exhausting. Still, my energy was heightened by crossing into another world.

At the ranch, we were immediately informed of two facts: The generator had just broken down, so there was no electricity; and a boa constrictor had that afternoon eaten the manager's pet deer. In this atmosphere of chaos I was shown to my room and, with only a few candles found and lit, I stumbled in the dark toward the bathroom.

Fortunately, the chaos did not prevent Luisa from going into the room before me with a flashlight. I heard her yell, "José, the machete!" followed by a whack. I watched as the body of a fairly small snake that had been curled on the back of my toilet was tossed out of the bathroom into my bedroom. Luisa used the tip of the machete to drop the dead snake into a burlap bag. As she left the room, she looked back and said in a quiet, easy voice, "Be careful; that deadly *fer de lance* snake loves water," and then added, "Our supper will soon be ready on the patio." Stuck in a stunned stance for several minutes, I decided I didn't need that particular bathroom, at least not that night.

The delicious Colombian soup, *ajiaco*—which I examined suspiciously for anything resembling a chicken's head—and a local pinto bean dish were served at a colorful table overlooking the fields of the plains. Luisa's casual manner and wild hair belied the complex explanation she offered of her research, which she attached to tales of the scientists' experiments.

"Look at all these little frogs surrounding us," I said with curiosity to the table.

"Oh, yes, but keep your feet away from them. They are the biting frogs," Luisa warned.

"What? Those innocent frogs with their tiny, sweet-looking mouths?" I murmured with a short laugh and a flash of a memory: As a fast-moving child in Central Park, I was constantly warned, "Don't run up the hill into those trees; the squirrels will bite you." More sweet-looking but dangerous—perhaps even deadly—animals seemed to be everywhere.

I looked down at my sandals and thought I'd best get the sneakers out of my bag. Perhaps socks, too, especially as I then learned it was the season of "no-see-ums," the tiny little gnats that burrow under your skin and cause dangerous and itchy welts.

The frog talk caused Bill and me to glance at each other and burst into "you must be kidding" guffaws. "We haven't been here an hour and you've told us—

The Soup With The Chicken's Eyes

or we've seen at least—four menacing threats. Where are we? Is this the 'Ranch of Fatal Encounters?'" Bill asked. Luisa laughed, unlike my New York cockroach-killer.

Bill and I discussed some specific *llanos* photographs he wanted for his business brochure, but he didn't want to stay at the ranch. "This is too much; I want to get out of here," he announced. In fact, he left two days later for his home in Bogotá. The young American mother would also soon leave, as the no-see-um bites put her and her baby in the hospital. I stayed on for a week with a heightened yet admittedly fearful curiosity. Having traveled for quite a while and developed my images along the way, and with a head full of questions, I wanted to remain and experience this wild place, if I could survive it. And anyway, I had told my new friend, Luisa, that I would help her make a small garden.

She and I began to talk about the impact of the Ranch of Fatal Encounters one afternoon on a fishing expedition at a nearby lake. I had jumped from our small boat to a spot of land in order to tie the boat to a tree, but my landing slurped me into mud up past my knees. I panicked. Luisa panicked. It wasn't quicksand, but the sucking power of the mud certainly felt like it. She threw me a rope and pulled and pulled as I slid my way out of trouble, panting all the while.

We sat in the boat wiping the mud off my now-caked khaki pants and began to giggle nervously.

"Luisa, Luisa, what's going on?" I demanded. "Nature certainly wins here. Please tell me why you're so attracted to this place, all this danger? You're about thirty, will you soon be moving on?"

"Well, you know," she started off slowly, "I'm from Medellín. It's a small city, a nice city, but I always felt closed in. I studied at the university; most of my courses were about nature. I wanted to be with the animals, so whenever I could I went to the wild areas of Colombia. Yes, nature is definitely in power here, in control, I should say"—she laughed—"but in truth, nature's power is everywhere, don't you think? We humans just believe we're in control. And this is where I feel most alive: the earthy smells of the animals, even the monkeys;

the heat, the humid air, the dangers; I like it. In an odd way, I feel safe here. Does that sound strange?"

Luisa turned off the motor so that we could listen to the howling of the monkeys. "This is the monkeys' time. Hear them speak."

"And you," she asked a few moments later, "you're a bit younger, in your twenties somewhere. Why are *you* here? Where do *you* feel alive and comfortable with who you are?"

"When I'm engaged with people," I answered. "I thought I was here for the adventure and, of course, for my photography. But it seems more than that. I have a big curiosity; people fascinate me. Hitchhiking south from Cartagena a few weeks ago, I was picked up by a young man who invited me to his mother's home for tea. She asked me what I'd seen in her country, what were important moments for me and why." I told Luisa about the outdoor Bogotá market that I'd been photographing to see what people buy, how they bargain, things like that. And I followed a man whose disabled child lay on the floor beside his food and basket stall. I watched his care for the child, sometimes interrupting the selling of his wares, and asked if I might photograph them for a few hours a day. He said yes.

"Those are some of the times that made me feel alive and connected."

Luisa nodded thoughtfully but didn't respond.

"My growing-up life was so far removed from *this* earthy, raw world," I continued. "I told you about my encounter with the chicken's eyes, how I wondered if hidden behind my curiosity was a false bravado that had been exposed. *Your* questions are asked and answered by animals and nature. *Mine* were asked by the chicken's eyes but are not yet answered."

"And the questions are what?"

"Oh, simply, the grand question of, 'Who am I?' "

We laughed.

"Oh, *that* question," Luisa answered solemnly.

"Another response to your 'alive' question is that I like adventures, testing myself to go further, to cross over into other territories, their people and cultures.

The Soup With The Chicken's Eyes

Some of it might be just a dare to myself. But even though I feel present in most of those experiences, I don't want to stay. I want to move on to the next experience. And so I question my motives. Am I just a voyeur, a wanderer, unable to fit in?"

"A dilemma for you, I see." Luisa answered slowly. "Perhaps you should be with the animals and nature, like me. There you will know that you'll never really fit in, never belong or . . . yes, well, you *will* belong, but only part-time. A sense of balance might be the answer for you: Accept your 'outsider' self, as a witness, as photographers often are, but know you are also present, not fearful of your own experience." She paused. "Your interest here at the ranch and your work in the garden proves that.

"That's my two-bit philosophy," Luisa added with a laugh. "And, if that doesn't make sense, come back and speak to the monkeys."

My job at the ranch in the mornings was to clean the blood from the neck of the horse I was given to ride. He was bitten every night by a vampire bat. There it was again, I said to myself: The bats are in power. The thought brought back a terrifying childhood memory. I was one of those children who believed that bats flying around would eventually get entangled in my hair. When I heard this particular ranch story, the nightmare resurfaced. "Vampire bats? What? I thought they just existed in the movies. This is too much," I exclaimed to Ricardo, the ranch foreman.

"Yes, they also exist here. Nature, she's strong in this part of the world. And I know someone who had a bat in their hair," he casually answered.

When he asked if I wanted to watch the bats get flushed from the hollow of a tree by fire, I exclaimed again, "You must be kidding!" and hurriedly but politely walked away. "Okay, another time; the bats will always return," he called after me with a quick laugh.

The conversation, the questions I'd asked Luisa, merged into a positive pile.

I found Ricardo the next day and asked him when we would flush the bats from the tree.

With surprise, he answered, "Oh, you've changed . . . I thought you didn't like . . . well, okay, this afternoon, over there, the tree by the barn."

I met Ricardo at the appointed hour. He lit a torch and stuck it in the tree hollow. The screeching bats swooshed out in droves, wide wings creating a chorus of deafening flutters. Their ugliness was pure horror to me. I stood as still as I could and stared at them, my feet poised to run.

With an image of the chicken's eyes flashing in my memory, I made myself watch the bats fly away, onward. I heard Luisa say, "Belonging is part-time."

XIII

CROSSING OVER

The Man in Bombay

I emerged from an underground tunnel onto the streets of Bombay. At the top of the stairs on the pavement was a gracefully positioned man, lying on his side on a flattened burlap sack. In front of him was piled a small mound of clothes and several books. I stopped, and on first glance, I saw a man of probably fifty. He was the image of peace and elegance in the midst of a raging city teeming with dirt, sickness, and all kinds of crawling things.

I could see a few well-worn books, and at the top of his stack was a book with an English title.

The man had a beautiful grey and white crop of hair, combed back to show a handsome, serene face accentuated by a soft grey beard. His eyes were closed, but he didn't seem to be sleeping. A long, dark blue man's shirt known as a *kurta* neatly covered his body to his knees, accentuating the beige Indian-style pants fitting his legs. His left hand was quietly draped over one leg. I could see he was wearing what looked like a gold signet ring on the fourth finger of his right hand, a hand that did not look like that of a laborer.

People streamed past him or stepped around him. Some gave him a glance, but his place on the street was secure; he seemed untroubled in an odd way. My friend, Ali, and I stood and stared.

He wasn't a beggar; there was no bowl, just books. Why had he chosen this particular spot? How did he retain this dignity? Did he represent a way of being in a world I didn't understand, a world of opposites?

I could have approached him and somehow asked, how did you get here? Why do you want to lie in this spot? Aren't you scared someone will step on

you, fall on you, take your books? What are those books? I wondered if the familiar street noise brought him some sort of peace.

But I didn't want to cross over the invisible barrier between us. I didn't want him to put his thoughts into a language that I might understand; that would have broken the spell. He was a mystery. I was an observer, and I wanted my fantasies to remain intact.

Hong Kong
"Do you like to dance?" asked the young, good-looking Englishman working in Hong Kong's financial district.

"Yes, I like to dance."

We didn't know each other, this nephew, named Paul, of an older friend in New York. She knew I would be spending a few days in Hong Kong and wanted me to see the exotic side of life there. "I know you well enough, even though

Crossing Over

you're only eighteen, to know you're not a tourist, you want to enter the side story. And then you can go on to meet your parents in Tokyo, not so exotic, I don't think. Hong Kong is a city of mystery. I lived there for ten years; you'll see."

The loud chatter of language and the banging sounds of vendors along the narrow streets gave a rush to my whole body, alive to this place. I drew in the earthy smells of the steamed fish and gave a thought to the cod and the whole chickens hanging in the windows.

Paul and I headed through an evening mist among the crowds that still moved fast, even at nine at night. The sweep of the overhead street signs made a colorful umbrella. Through the fog, I could see the water and hear the slap of the boats against the docks as an occasional lonely foghorn warned the overly crowded harbor.

Paul took my arm and pointed to seedy and crooked descending steps. It was dark and I held onto the old bamboo railing with trust and anticipation. A few steps down and I could hear the sultry music and smell the heavy cigarette smoke wafting up the stairs. After another few steps, I caught a glimpse of women languidly swirling in their long, silk, slit-up-both-sides *cheongsams*. The dresses were as sensual as the music.

"That's the erhu, the haunting Chinese fiddle, driving the tone," he offered. "It has magic in it, don't you think?"

"Yes, yes, I'm in its swirling dizziness." I attempted a laugh.

We sat on the edge of the dancing circle. "And, no, I'm not quite ready to dance," I offered. "Perhaps a Scotch, isn't that what everyone drinks here?"

"Yes," he said with a laugh, "and a lot of it."

After several whiskeys, we danced. We moved around the space in a glide, but our glide was awkward compared to the women in their *cheongsams* brushing past me, some bent into a slight curve as their male partners gently leaned over them. I want that, I thought. Would an Asian man dance with me like that? No, I answered myself. They were good dancers, but that wasn't the only magic. It was the place, the smoke, the hypnotic allure of a beckoning world, a voluptuous atmosphere, enticing perhaps because it seemed unreachable.

The Man and His Cello

In the West Village in New York, on the corner of Bleeker and 10th, a musician sat on an upturned box playing his cello. That corner was familiar to me, as there used to be a bar on the opposite corner that always had very cool music for slow dancing. We went there a lot at the end of a fast work day at my nonprofit entity on Wall Street; the bar had felt sensuous and serene and lazy.

The cellist's particular corner was quiet, no hustle and bustle, especially at that late hour. I walked across the narrow street to stand and listen, but not so close as to disturb him. He finished and looked at me with soft, serious blue eyes.

"What are you playing?" I asked. "It's a prelude, but I can't think of the name."

"Oh yes, I am practicing the prelude to the Bach suites."

"And may I ask, why do you practice right here, on the street?"

"Because here I am within the world, *my* world of music. I sit and play and know people can hear me, but they are not obliged to stop, and I, too, am not obliged to stop playing. I am with them but I am alone."

"I believe I know that feeling. You allow us to be in your world and yet we and you can also remain in our own worlds?"

"Yes, exactly," he answered wistfully. "Ah, so many worlds."

He smiled, looked down at his cello, and began the prelude again.

Crossing Over

The Millenium

On the last afternoon of 1999, I heard an ominous warning bellowing from the TV: *There's going to be a cyberattack throughout the world on January 1st, New Year's Day. Don't get on airplanes, there's danger ahead; be careful.*

I sat on my friend's bed in New York watching and hearing the TV amidst the sounds of New Year celebrations around the world.

Near eight in the evening, I looked forward to celebrating the millennium's momentous occasion at a black-tie dinner with my good friend Sean and his friends, a lively group from different parts of the world. Since Sean owned a famous New York catering company, I anticipated a fantastic dinner.

My plane ticket from New York via Albuquerque to my home in Santa Fe was for January 2. But an urgent desire kept coming up as I watched the disturbing news, the warning: I wanted to be in Santa Fe in the afternoon of New Year's Day so I could attend the late afternoon candlelight service at Pajarito, the small chapel at the foot of the spiritually evocative Black Mesa. How could I do that unless I defied the warning and travelled tomorrow?

My two worlds—New York City and Santa Fe—had a mysticism. I longed to take in both, to know the mysteries of the two experiences, even more so if this could be the end of the world.

I called the airlines. May I exchange my ticket from my flight that I have on January 2 to tomorrow, January 1? Is there something in the early morning to Albuquerque?

"Yes, easy," said the reservations agent. "There's a flight from LaGuardia at 8 a.m., getting you into Albuquerque at 2:30 in the afternoon."

"I'll take it."

We went to Sean's friend Klaus's apartment for dinner: hot crab soup, a tenderloin with a spicy horseradish sauce, exotic vegetables, great red wine; then a sweet wine that I didn't like arrived with the chocolate mousse. Toasts, thoughts for a new beginning—what would come to us in 2000?

"I predict world unity," Sean's English friend said with an unusual optimism.

At 11:30, with bottles of Champagne under our arms and plastic cups in our coat pockets, we crossed through Central Park to the West Side of town for a party. The heels I wore didn't bother me—no snow. The chimes struck twelve as we passed the park's skating rink, causing a yell of millennial celebration. It seemed everyone who had Champagne was passing it around with kisses. I saw one man throw his skating partner up in the air and she twisted around in a graceful loop.

Walking through the throngs, I felt an intimacy in the midst of strangers.

We arrived at the party. Sean, who had won the Irish jig contest at a New York Irish bar at age twelve, performed it again. We stood on a small balcony close enough to hear the roaring revelry in Times Square. More Champagne, more kisses from strangers. The energy, the warmth, the optimism, the sudden friendships in a crowd; at that moment, I was sure they would last forever. Why not?

"Oh no, it's 2 a.m., how will we get home?" I worried aloud. "I bet there are no taxis, but a bus must be going across town."

"No charge on the millennium night," announced the bus driver with a smile. "You people out there, just get on the bus and we'll go," he shouted with a laugh.

I had already packed my suitcase. With the hope that just enough sleep would get me to the airport in Albuquerque and on to Santa Fe to pick up my dog, Harry, I felt a surge of a thrill for tomorrow's crossing from New York's exhilarating energy over into the rural otherworld of New Mexico. Two worlds: How could it be better than this?

Only three people were on the plane. The flight attendant said we could sit up front in first class.

"The Universe told me I was supposed to be on this plane," I said to her. "If this is the end, then this trip is filled with magic." She laughed but looked at me with a curious expression.

I stopped at my house in Santa Fe, put on warm clothes and picked up Harry for the half-hour drive north to Pajarito. I had found him—tiny, abandoned and freezing—two years ago on a dirt road outside Chama. I knew when I grabbed him to take him home that his full name would be "Highway Harry."

Crossing Over   119

But from then on Harry wouldn't get in a car until the day I was moving to a different house, and he apparently knew he had to chance it. He waited for me, crammed into a tiny space on the back seat floor. He and I moved to the new house together.

Black Mesa looks like a soft sponge. The simple but formidable mound emerges from the ground into a flat brown, beige and black surface. That afternoon, the mound seemed to alter with the fading light.

The little adobe church, with its view of the mystical mesa, probably holds only fifty people. I quietly squeezed into a pew in the back, feeling myself an outsider—but not an intruder, as the mostly Hispanic/Native American group gave me a nod. I had a temporary feeling of belonging. I knew the church a bit as I had worked there as a "mudder," a volunteer mission church restorer. We would come up to the village with plaster, buckets and drop cloths to re-mud the exterior walls. One of the rewards was an enchilada and *sopapilla* lunch given by the community. Another reward of the mudding was being able to throw the wet earth, with full force, at an exterior wall that we all imagined as an enemy.

Coats, hats and scarves were piled on the floor by the pews. A guitar player started off the service. The words of the songs and the prayers, all in Spanish, were written on pieces of paper handed out at the door. The altar at the front of the chapel was plain; a large cross loomed behind it. No electricity, but candlelight—big ones at the altar, small votives on the side aisles—gave the space a dreamy glow. I could see wisps of falling snow through several of the windows, and soon I heard the snow turn to hail on the roof, a rhythm I thought matched the singing.

As the prayers, homily and hymns came to an end, we stood in that kind of peace that is unfocused. Filing out with the help of the moonlight, I felt somehow invited into the mystery of the Black Mesa. Families hugged each other; some included me.

While Pajarito's single bell rang out, I thought of the jubilant bells I heard coming from a church near Central Park at midnight the night before. One sound had been boisterous, one was serene.

I liked both.

Dancing in Brazil

In the hot sun of late afternoon, two Brazilian friends and I walked down a sand and dirt road on the coast of their country. The heat made me lazy; I had little energy to empty my sandals of the irritating small pebbles stuck under my feet.

We turned a few corners and pulled ourselves up a small hill that gave a glimpse of the sea. I heard music, or was it the heat creating a mirage of sounds down the way? No, it was from the barn. We quickened our steps to reach the sensuous samba music, the soul-beating sounds that come up through one's legs in waves. Entering into a mass of swirling colors—arms raised, red toenails on bare feet, men in thin-threaded white shirts and pants, and women in multihued skirts, scarves gracefully flying—we melded into the dancers, each in our own dreamy rhythm, in twos, alone; even the barn seemed to sway with the beat.

I remembered the night in the Hong Kong bar and my uneasy witnessing of the dancers, envying their unselfconscious moves.

Tonight I looked down at my dancing feet becoming part of the magic.

Photograph was taken by a Russian colleague in Kosovo

Joan Brooks Baker is a native New Yorker who has made her home in Santa Fe, New Mexico, since 1982. Her photographs have been exhibited in galleries in both cities and at the United Nations. She now calls herself "a photographer writing."

ACKNOWLEDGEMENTS - WITH THANKS

To Margeaux Klein, my life partner, and to my always positive sister, Alice

To my extraordinary publisher and designer with a most beautiful "eye", Nancy Stem/ Fresco Books, my creative editor, Hollis Walker, and to my forever patient helper in all things, Wendy Young

For the opinions and critiquers: Laura Yorke, Carol Mancusi Ungaro-Steen, the "So What" writing group: Felice Gonzalez, Mary Frank Sanborn, Anna Jastrzembski and Debra Weiner, Elisabeth Reed, Cecile Lipworth, Nancy Wirth, Susan and Trenholm Walker, Nikko, Susan Herter, Katie Kitchen and Paul Kovach, David Hawkanson, Pattie Sullivan, Leana Melat, Ann Yeomans, Kristine Rael, Jo Parfitt and the writers of The Windmill, Magda Bogin and the writers of Under the Volcano, Lisa Barlow, Louisa Sarofim, Kate Harrington, Nan Newton, Dorothy Massey, Dusty Rhodes, Raashan Ahmed, Stefan Anderman, Jane Lahr, Liz Glassman, Anne Gallagher, Kathryn and Roger Toll, Bonnie Joseph, Sharon Fernandes, Andree and Donald Smith, Linda Durham, Julia Bergen, Alexandra Eldridge, Mae Martinez, Jessica Guilford of the Santa Fe Public Library, Sallie Bingham, Betsy Barlow and Ted Rogers, Singer Rankin and my long-time friends: Joe Wemple, Lee Link, Victoria Shorr and Louise Whitney